A Katama Bay Christmas

A KATAMA BAY SERIES

KATIE WINTERS

Chapter One

The Manhattan Reproductive Medicine Clinic was located on E. 74th Street, just east of Central Park and mere blocks from the apartment where Maggie Potter had grown up as the prestigious and well-off daughter of oil tycoon Jack Potter. Now, years away from any reality she could understand, she hovered in the rain outside of the clinic itself as swarms of memories overtook her.

She could practically see the three of them: Jack, Maggie, and her younger sister, Alyssa, as they rushed excitedly through these same streets, en route for intellectual conversations over milkshakes or long afternoons at The Met. Their father had always demanded more of their minds and belittled them in small ways if they'd taken to giggles. Even still, the girls had adored those afternoons with their father, especially given the fact that he was so often out of town on business or at one meeting after another.

Only a month ago, Jack Potter's heart— something Maggie and Alyssa had assumed was black as night and incapable of faltering, had spontaneously stopped beating. The aftermath was something Maggie knew would tear through her for the rest of her life.

She was only twenty-five years old— an age the internet told her was "completely viable" and "appropriate" for child-birth. Why, then, did she stand at the double-wide doors of the highly-recommended Manhattan Fertility Clinic, on the verge of some kind of mental breakdown?

The rain flattened itself across her umbrella and cast down around her to join the Manhattan puddles. Her boots were damp, her toes sharp with cold. She scanned the far corners of the street for signs of her husband, Rex, who had agreed to meet her outside the clinic at 2:45 sharp. As a prestigious businessman with a stacked calendar of meetings, Rex had asked to slip the appointment between two work events. Maggie had wanted to offer a sharp-tongued reply, something to the effect of, "Oh, I see you'll just slip our child in between your other, more important meetings?" She had felt echoes of her father in those choice words and regretted them immediately.

But Rex wasn't like her father. Her reaction towards him was simplistic in its child-like nature. She was just frightened.

At 2:49, another woman bustled out from the double-wide doors of the clinic. Maggie deflated her umbrella and stepped into the foyer, which was grey and soothing and dry. The receptionist wore large-frame glasses and greeted her with soft tones. Every woman who entered the doors of the fertility clinic was in the midst of a low-grade nightmare. They had to be handled with care.

"The doctor will see you shortly," the receptionist told her. "Please have a seat."

Maggie and Rex had already been to this clinic two weeks

previously, just before Thanksgiving. Rex had resisted the idea, saying that they just needed to "try harder." Maggie had protested and used facts to back it up. They hadn't used any form of birth control since summertime, a couple of months prior to their wedding. They'd called it an "experiment" and decided that if they did get pregnant (which seemed almost a sure thing at the time), it was meant to be. They'd both wanted a family and had even spoken about it on their first date. They saw no reason to wait.

One month had seemed reasonable. Two had seemed fine. Three had brought confusion. Now, nearly six months into trying, Maggie ached with desperation and fear. Had she done something wrong? The internet suggested that a woman of her age wait a full year before seeking outside treatment. Maggie, however, was a doer, not a waiter— and she had the funds to back up her needs. The fertility specialist had completed many tests on her, along with Rex's sperm. She and Rex had joked they were a part of a strange scientific experiment. The joke didn't seem so funny, but it was all they had.

Only a few weeks before, Maggie had confessed to her mother that she and Rex were "finally ready" to conceive; she'd hoped verbalizing their desires would will a pregnancy forward. Still, when her mother had shown such excitement, Maggie had felt the universe mocking her. You couldn't play games with the universe and expect decent outcomes.

Minutes ticked past. Maggie texted Rex to ask where he was. The message gave her only a single check-mark in response, proof that his phone was either dead or off. She shivered with a chill.

Fertility and adoption magazines lined the corner tables within the clinic. The adoption magazine's front cover featured an older mother, her hair lined attractively with grey and white. She held a little baby from an Asian country and gave a secretive smile to the camera, as though she'd discovered something with motherhood that others couldn't guess. When Rex had suggested adoption as a viable option, Maggie's heart had shattered. Would her body really give up on her like this? She'd always been able to count on it before.

"Maggie Potter? The doctor will see you, now."

Maggie stepped through the taupe-painted hallway and entered the mahogany doorway of Dr. Shellac, a woman oft-touted as the number-one fertility doctor in all of Manhattan. When Rex had suggested they meet with a Brooklyn-based doctor, Maggie had protested and found her father's opinions within her. Only Manhattan was best.

"Good afternoon, Maggie," Dr. Shellac began. Her nails were trimmed tight against her fingers, and her horn-rimmed glasses were like a professor's from the seventies. She was forty-five, maybe, and word had it she'd delivered twin babies from IVF two years before, at forty-three. There were no photographs as proof.

"Good afternoon. If you don't mind, perhaps we could wait a few minutes for my husband? He's coming in from a meeting."

Dr. Shellac didn't flinch. "Unfortunately, my schedule is too tight to wait. We could arrange another meeting for you to go over the results."

Maggie imagined the death march of waiting for the next appointment. It was always better to know rather than hover in the in-between. Wasn't it?

"Okay." Maggie swallowed the lump in her throat. "I'd prefer to know now, I suppose."

Dr. Shellac clicked through a tab on her computer. Silence fell

4

over them. Maggie said a silent prayer. How easy would it be for Dr. Shellac to just say, *"Everything looks great! Just keep trying."*

"So, we investigated your and your husband's fertility, both separately and when paired together, as sometimes, two systems just don't operate well together for fertility."

Maggie's nostrils flared.

"We found that your husband's sperm count is healthy. Everything looks good in his regard. But your results are a bit different. We found a number of complications, including Polycystic Ovary Syndrome and a uterine abnormality which makes it much harder for your egg to latch to the uterine walls."

Maggie's lips parted in shock. The doctor's tone was soft and mellow, but the words were akin to gunfire.

"What are you saying?" Why did it feel as though the walls crashed in on her from every direction?

"You're only..." Dr. Shellac glanced back at her chart for reference. "You're only twenty-five. I imagine this is quite hard to hear at your age."

"I assumed it would be easy."

Dr. Shellac nodded. "Pregnancy is a complicated thing, and your body simply isn't built for it."

"Isn't there something I can do?" Maggie hardly recognized her voice. It sounded breathy and strange.

"There are ways. IVF has been seen to work in your case. This can be a rather grueling process, but one that very well could lead you to pregnancy success."

IVF? Maggie's throat tightened. The vague ideas she had around it involved needles, multiple egg production and sperm inserted into her egg in some lab somewhere. No passion. No love. Just sterile equipment.

"I don't know. Maybe... maybe we can keep trying?" Maggie whispered.

Dr. Shellac shook her head delicately. Her eyes shimmered but lacked sorrow. Probably, she had had this same conversation so many times already that day and would soon watch Maggie leave her office to have to say it all over again to someone else. Maggie was just another statistic.

"If you'd like, we can arrange an additional meeting to discuss IVF. Otherwise, you probably know there are many other options for potential parents. It's best not to limit yourself when it comes to the joy of parenting. We've made great strides in science— but there are a number of children out there in the wide world who really need a good home from loving people."

Maggie stood on quivering legs, thanked the doctor, and returned to the taupe hallway. The receptionist's nails clacked against the keyboard as she skirted past. She entered the bathroom and gaped at her reflection in the mirror, an image she was meant to know and understand. Her dark hair cascaded down her shoulders. Her eyes reflected the soft light, and her lipstick was perfect, the new autumn line from Estée Lauder she'd picked up recently on a shopping spree with her sister. Anyone who saw her on the streets of Manhattan or Brooklyn or Edgartown, Massachusetts, would have assumed her to be the kind of woman who "had it all."

Maggie stretched a hand over her stomach and tried to feel the unrest within her. For twenty-five years, her uterus had laid in wait in preparation to destroy her on this day in early December, one month after her father's death. "Good timing," she whispered to her reflection.

Maggie staggered back into the hallway and fished for her phone in her purse. Rex's message still hadn't gone through. She called her sister for some sign of life in the world, but when Alyssa answered, Maggie hurriedly said, "Oh sorry, I accidentally butt-dialed you." She hadn't told Alyssa anything about her fertility issues. It was a strange thing for Maggie and Alyssa to keep things from one another. They normally told one another everything.

But Alyssa's previous few weeks had been a whirlwind as well. She'd had an ill-fated romance with a Dutchman who'd lived on Martha's Vineyard, who'd tried to assault her on their father's airplane when Alyssa had decided, on a whim, they head to Spain.

"You butt-dialed me? What a pleasure," Alyssa teased sleepily.

"Are you asleep?" Maggie's voice was now bouncy and playful, a total contrast to her inner emotions.

"What? Sleeping? Why would I sleep in the middle of the day?" Mid way through her words, Alyssa erupted into a yawn. "Okay, okay. You caught me. I've been in the city since last night. Right now, I'm stitching together my hungover body with a nap and a bagel."

"Oh!" Maggie's heart lifted just the slightest bit. Since Alyssa had taken up near-full-time residence at her mother and grand-mother's house on the Vineyard, the city had felt strangely sinister and dark. "I had no idea you were around."

"Around and almost ready to rebound," Alyssa confirmed. "I'll call you in a bit. I'm going to do a hot yoga session down the road."

"Go sweat out those toxins, girl," Maggie responded brightly. "Love you."

"Ditto!"

Maggie shoved her phone back into her pocket and stepped toward the door that led back out onto 74th St. The spitting rain had transformed to a soft, cascading snow, the delicate sort that melted upon your shoulders the moment it landed. As she stepped out into the grey light, a tear slipped down her cheek. She was jealous of the version of herself Alyssa still assumed her to be, the version of herself who still didn't know her body would fail her in such an awful way.

Chapter Two

Linda Piper lived in a rent-controlled apartment in lower Manhattan and had so for years since her depressive episodes had made it borderline impossible to keep up her life of travel. For decades, it had been her joy in life to accept jobs across the world. She had worked as a waitress at a lodge in Alaska, a cook at the scientific outpost in Antarctica, a caregiver for the elderly in England, a newspaper delivery girl in France, a phone operator in China, and other silly odd jobs, from coast to coast and beyond. The depressive episodes had been like internal hurricanes of sorrow, starting around the age of forty-one or forty-two, and had grown exponential in their power. Now, at sixty-five, she clung to each moment of relative happiness for dear life, knowing full-well that it could be her last, at least for a while.

Linda's apartment had been almost the same since her move-in fifteen years before. She had a single bed beneath a tiny window, which offered space only enough for her, as she never required any additional space for any extra people (men had left her life a long, long time ago). She had a single kettle on the stove-top, colored bright red, and a small table with two rickety-looking chairs, both of which she'd selected from the street after someone had left them there on moving day. A calendar hung on the kitchen wall, which she marked X's across to note the passage of time.

Every morning, including this one, Linda ate the same break-fast: cream of wheat with a single cup of tea. She then read for twenty minutes from a romance novel, showered, brushed her hair, and dressed in a pair of jeans and a sweater. Normally, she prayed for the early shift at her retail position, which meant she had somewhere to go first. If she had the later shift, like today, she was trapped. What was there to do with herself?

Linda's work began at four and ran till ten. Beforehand, she decided to don her winter coat and walk the streets of Manhattan, feeling the snow as it kissed her cheeks gently and melted across her shoulders. She allowed herself to glide into the backdrop of the city where she had grown up, to become just another mechanism amid traffic and wild horn blasts and shuffling pedestrians. During her final job away from the city, which had been in Death Valley, where she'd worked as a waitress at a roadside diner, one of her co-workers had asked her where she planned to go. "Back to the city, of course," had been Linda's answer. "But won't you be lonely there?" the girl had asked. "You're never lonely in the city. You just have to look around and see hundreds of people around you," Linda had returned.

She still believed that, although it was all a matter of perspec-tive. It was true that she had very few connections within the city. Her parents were dead, and she'd never managed to re-contact her old friends upon her return, as she'd felt too much had happened in-between. *Besides, hadn't she had enough fun in her life? Did she truly deserve friendship?*

It was almost Christmas. The streets were decorated, just as they always were, with strings of lights, bright red bows, and fake lines of greenery. With the snowfall swirling around her, Linda could imagine herself in a Christmas fantasy. Only her somber, aching heart brought her back down to reality.

About nine months ago, Linda had begun work at a high-end retailer in Manhattan, where she assisted incredibly wealthy Manhattan women on their quest to be "well-dressed" and "better than their peers." It was a competition among the socialites to be nothing but the best. Linda herself had never had much money, but she did have expensive taste. As a younger woman in London, Paris, and Tokyo, she had scrambled through second-hand retailers to pick up the latest fashions by top designers. When she'd explained this to Connie, manager at "DENISE," Connie had offered her the job on the spot. "There's something about you I can't place," she'd said at the time. "Something high-society Manhattan women will appreciate. You blend into the background until you're absolutely needed."

Linda approached the boutique twenty minutes before her shift. Just outside the door, a young mother in a periwinkle blue winter coat bent down to fix the buttons of her young daughter's coat. A winter wind erupted through the streets and whisked the young girl's hat from her head, which caused it to tumble across the pavement and land in front of Linda's feet. She bent down, grabbed it and flailed it through the air for the mother to see.

"Oh goodness," the young mother said as she righted herself and hustled for the hat. "Thank you so much."

Linda could hardly look at her. She was fascinated with the

beautiful young girl before her. "How old is your daughter?" she asked as she gave the hat back.

"Four," the young girl answered for herself. She snuck the hat back on her head with finality.

"That's a great age," Linda affirmed. Memories spiked through her, as jagged as knives.

Moments like this always threatened to take her all the way down into the depths of her depression. She righted herself, smiled sadly, and then whisked herself into DENISE, where classical music folded over her with familiarity and the manager, Connie, waved to her from the cash register.

"Hello, Linda. We received a new order this morning. So many beautiful clothes. I hope you're ready to push them!" Connie's long earrings wiggled as she spoke, distracting her.

"Wonderful to hear," Linda tried, although her smile hardly reached her eyes. "I'll head back and take a look."

Linda eased into the dark shadows of the back hallway and storage rooms, where she discovered the new boxes of clothing, all of which would have to be sorted and placed on the racks in the best-possible, most-sellable positions. It was essential to please the eye of the buyer or even someone on the street. Window shopping wasn't yet a dead medium, not in Manhattan, and spontaneous purchases sometimes tended to be the biggest.

Linda returned to the front counter, where Connie conversed with a high-end customer who carried a Birkin bag. Linda headed for the front of the store again to ensure everything was lined up properly and all the sizes were in the correct order. Another customer entered, whom Linda greeted warmly before the customer promptly ignored her and texted someone on her phone. It was never easy to gauge how much a customer wanted help. Often, they wanted to be left alone, but Connie insisted Linda always engage them.

The endless ignoring-of-Linda seemed to extend out from the store and into the wide world. It was just nature's course, especially now, at her age. Women over fifty didn't get the attention they deserved and after sixty? Don't even think about it.

Connie headed out for an hour around five-thirty, leaving Linda alone in the store for a good half-hour. Foot traffic normally picked up around six-fifteen as people finished their jobs and headed to meet friends for dinner. That rush extended to around eight when the traffic dwindled toward their nine-thirty close.

Linda was starved, as she had only eaten her cream of wheat for breakfast and neglected her traditional soup for lunch. Connie was on a perpetual diet, but kept various snacks at the counter just in case her blood sugar was low. Linda sifted through little packs of almonds and low-carb granola bars, but nothing called out to her. To the right of the snack-pile sat a selection of gossip magazines, which Connie confessed to reading in secret when patrons weren't in the store.

Linda wasn't so keen on gossip. However, she liked to see what the high-society women wore to various functions, as they gave her ideas on how to market to the ladies within the shop. As she scanned and sifted through the glossy pages, she discovered a large-block-lettered headline which read:

JACK POTTER'S WIFE AND MISTRESS REUNITED

Linda's heart quickened. The headline was for a story on page forty-seven, which she hurriedly flipped toward. There, she found a photograph of Maxine Aubert and Janine Grimson Potter, two

Manhattan millionaire socialites who had started out as poor Brooklyn girls before their rise in status.

According to the magazine, which was fueled by gossip (but normally found its way toward facts), Janine and Maxine had reunited as friends after the untimely death of Janine's husband, Jack Potter. Janine had discovered Jack and her best friend, Maxine, had been having an affair back in May, which naturally led to the end of their decades-long friendship. However, in the wake of Jack's death, "sources report having seen Maxine Aubert at the Katama Lodge and Wellness Spa, where Janine works as a naturopathic doctor. The women have come to a sort of resolution and have decided to rebuild what they once had, which was a powerful friendship."

The magazine featured several far-away paparazzi shots of two women who seemed to be Janine and Maxine as they walked the streets of a beautiful-looking, quaint village called Edgartown, making their way in and out of boutiques. The women's style was on-point and their faces were vibrant with smiles.

How was it possible that Janine had found a way to forgive Maxine for what she'd done?

It seemed outside the bounds of reasonable thought.

Had Linda ever found it within herself to forgive in such a way? Had she ever received such forgiveness?

In reality, maybe, she hadn't stuck around long enough in any given place to actually work on her relationships. She hadn't had to forgive, and she hadn't had to be forgiven. *What did that mean?*

"Hey. Hello?" A sharp-nosed woman snapped her finger directly in Linda's face. "Are you there?"

Linda shook her head violently and made her grey-blonde

locks quake. "I'm terribly sorry. I drifted off for a moment. How can I help you?"

Linda couldn't remember the last time someone had snapped directly in her face before. It terrified her. It made her feel less than a human.

"I'm here for a very particular reason," the woman articulated. "I have several events over the holiday season and must be dressed appropriately for all. I've had luck in your boutique previously." She arched her back and lifted her chest forward, as though she wanted to flash her ultra-expensive broach in Linda's direction.

Linda shivered. "What sort of wardrobe did you have in mind?" She stepped around the counter and led the woman toward the back corner, where DENISE featured a fine selection of black-wear— long dresses with surging necklines or jumpsuits with well-placed details. The woman clucked her tongue with disdain.

"Perhaps you don't quite understand what I require," the woman snapped. "This sort of thing? It's basic. It's dull. It's assuredly what every other woman at these events will wear. But I'm not just any woman. I'm Margorie Besman and I'm meant to be noticed."

Linda wanted to articulate just how little she'd ever heard of Margorie Besman, but she figured that wasn't the kind of thing you did if you wanted to boost sales.

"Right this way," Linda replied instead as she led Margorie toward the front right-hand corner, where a selection of beige and taupe and teal dresses awaited. She flashed several to the front to display them better and discussed the sort of things they high-lighted. Throughout, Margorie just clucked her tongue.

"Again, I feel you're not hearing me," Margorie told her.

"Why don't we try over here?" Linda again guided her toward the back left-hand corner, where she showed off a glittery gold get-up that seemed both over-wrought and flashy.

Still, she could see Margorie wasn't so sure. "I've explained to you what sort of woman I am, have I not? Sophisticated. Ethereal. The sort of woman people in Manhattan look to with the assurance that..."

"That she'll be endlessly snobby and belittle them?" Linda blurted, even surprising herself.

Margorie's lips parted with shock. She wasn't accustomed to being spoken to like that. "I beg your pardon?"

Linda was just as surprised as Margorie, perhaps even more so. She wasn't accustomed to any kind of attitude from herself, either. As an awkward silence stretched between them, Connie arrived back from her break and greeted them brightly.

"Good evening! Welcome to DENISE."

Margorie yanked her perfect body around to glare at Connie. "Are you the manager?"

"I am." Connie's smile remained trained across her face. "Can I help you with something?"

"Yes. This employee here has spoken out of line." Margorie's nostrils flared as she stepped back so that her heel clacked against the ground.

Connie continued her focus on the customer. "I am sure I can help you with whatever you need."

"No. I believe you, too, have misunderstood what I just said," Margorie continued. "I have come to spend a considerable amount of money on outfits that I need, and I feel that..."

But as Margorie spoke, Linda's ears began to ring so intensely that she could no longer hear what Margorie said. It became muffled, as though she'd pressed her ear up against a wall to hear beyond it. Linda took several steps backward and collapsed against a clothing rack, which fell back behind her as she crumbled onto the floor. There was a cry of alarm, but Linda's only focus remained on the ceiling above her.

Where was she? What had she done?

Minutes passed, during which she spun with worries and fears but still couldn't move her small frame. After what seemed like a small eternity, her eyes found focus with the soft face of Connie. Connie spoke her name yet again, trying to draw her out from this other realm. But Linda felt far, far away from anything real.

What had happened? Why did she feel so useless, like nothing? Why did the world look at her like a speck of dust? Why did Linda feel on the verge of death all the time? And why had she been robbed of her single chance at happiness all those years ago?

"Come on, Linda. Breathe with me. Drink something, please." Linda blinked her eyes open to find Connie with a glass of water outstretched.

Slowly, Linda lifted her head and upper back to lean against a soft pile of clothes. She gripped the glass of water as, bit-by-bit, she returned to the earth. Her first sips allowed her to speak.

"What happened?"

Connie turned her head to glance back at the boutique, which was empty save for them. "You fainted. I don't know." She didn't sound pleased.

Linda squeezed her eyes shut for a split second as Connie patted her shoulder again.

"Come on, Linda. Let's get you back up. I don't want another customer to leave."

Linda tipped herself forward, gripped the counter, and hauled herself to a standing position. When she glanced in the mirror to the left, she saw a well-dressed sixty-five-year-old woman, her hair puffy from her fall and her eyes manic, as though she still lurked in another dimension, far, far away.

"Linda? Are you okay?" Connie looked at her with sharp-edged disdain.

"Yes, I think so. I'll be fine." This was yet another lie in a long stream of lies that Linda had told others and herself over the years. She was fine. She was always fine.

But after nine-thirty, when they flipped the OPEN sign to CLOSED, Connie led Linda into her back office and told her she had to let her go.

"You treated a customer poorly and created a bad ambiance," Connie explained formally. "Under no circumstances can I allow that to go on. It only takes one of those ladies to talk about their bad experience here to give us a bad name. I'm sure you understand."

Linda's throat tightened. She wanted to ask this woman what else she was meant to do with herself. She wanted to ask her how she was meant to pay her rent. She wanted to ask her what she, a woman of sixty-five, was meant to do for comfort in this cruel world.

But Connie had problems of her own. They were on far different treks of life. She had to do what she had to do.

"Thank you for this opportunity, Connie. I wish you well."

Linda rose, grabbed her coat, and gazed lovingly at the large stack of boxes from the new order. How she'd wanted to touch the new fabric with tender fingers; how she'd wanted to arrange the pieces artistically throughout the boutique.

How she'd wanted to arrive there every day for her shift, if only so her body had a place to go throughout the day.

Now what?

Linda returned to the street, which continued to swim with snowflakes. A young man across the road screamed at the sky while passers-by marched along, pretending not to notice. Linda wanted to join him. What was the point of human consciousness and empathy if it wasn't used? What was the point of money if she couldn't make it? What was the point of aging if all it did was make you sad and tired?

Linda continued her trek home as her shoulders slumped forward even more. Perhaps she was the loneliest woman in the world. But the worst thing about being the loneliest woman in the world was just how easily you slipped into that world, unnoticed. She could have been anyone— someone's mother, someone's best friend, someone's lover. But she was none of that. She felt utterly alone.

Chapter Three

I t was borderline incredible just how many people made time to have their own babies in a city as self-centered as New York. As Maggie hobbled down 74th street before making her turn south toward Brooklyn, she was amazed at the sheer number of babies she witnessed. They buzzed their lips at her from their chest-carriers, tucked against their mother or father's chest; they bugged their eyes out at her from buggies that passed by; they even waved to her, now and again, as though they wanted to mock her for her inability to create one of her own. *Was this always what Manhattan was like? Or was it only this way when you were singularly depressed about your own infertility?*

Before their marriage, Maggie and Rex had walked the streets of New York City on some sort of vendetta to discover every inch of the other's psyche. No topic seemed too outlandish. They'd talked about everything from the proper way to make grilled cheese sandwiches to how they wanted to raise their children to how they would deal with it when their parents died. (Obviously, when Jack Potter had passed away, Maggie had found that her original ideas around the fact had very little to do with reality. In fact, grief had no valid route forward.)

Now, as she marched through the streets alone, Maggie felt a heaviness upon her shoulders that she seemed unable to shake. She gripped her designer purse with a gloved hand and tried to focus her attention on her feet, cursing her belief in high-heeled boots no matter the occasion. Perhaps going forward, when she was about to receive crippling news, she would plan to wear flats or sneakers.

And in truth, there was no reason on earth that she now continued to walk. All that money in her trust fund and she refused to call a taxi? But the ache of her heart seemed to diminish as she marched along the road alone. Maybe this is how she was meant to be. Maybe she hadn't spent enough time within herself over the years. Maybe she'd jumped into love too soon.

Maybe— just maybe— she'd never been meant to be a mother. Maybe she was being punished for something she did. She didn't know the answers, only the facts.

But no! That had been her only dream of the previous few years. The other stuff, working in various art galleries around the city, had been garnish on an otherwise near-perfect existence. She loved art; she loved her career. But she wanted to build the love within her and Rex's home all the more— squabbling babies and silly songs and long, exhausting nights of putting sick ones to bed. She wanted it all.

"Hey, girl." It was Alyssa again, calling from another realm. "I just left hot yoga."

How long had it been? Maggie blinked up at the street sign,

which read 33rd street. She'd walked over forty blocks in the snow. She couldn't remember a time she'd ever done that.

"Hey! What's up?"

"Me and a few friends want to go out in a little while. Do you want to join us?"

"Didn't you just get over your hangover?"

Alyssa giggled. "Come on, sis. It's Christmas."

"It's December 5th. It's hardly Christmas."

"Well, I play good girl all the time on the island. I need to live it up in the city before I head back tomorrow and I want you there along with me— and Rex, if he isn't playing super-businessman again."

Maggie's stomach twisted with sorrow. Rex still hadn't reached out to her. He'd missed one of the most important meetings of their young lives as a couple. What else would he miss? Would he transform into a man similar to Jack Potter? Would he meet a similar fate?

"Sure. I'm down," Maggie finally replied. "Which bar?"

"Yours Sincerely. That place on Wilson," Alyssa told her. "Where are you, anyway? It sounds loud."

"I'm still in Manhattan," Maggie affirmed.

"Oh god. Get out of there."

Maggie hung up, then slipped her phone in her pocket and realized with a funny flip in her gut that her father's grave was close to where she now stood. She hadn't been to visit since the burial, which had been tremendously painful, so much so that she'd almost blacked it out of her memory. Her knee twitched her rightward toward the cemetery as though guided by an unseen force. And in only a moment, she found herself at the outer edge of the stone monuments, those that represented decades of prominent Manhattan families, all long-dead.

A crinkly sunflower lay upon the soil over Jack Potter's coffin. Maggie wondered who'd left the mysterious flower. *An old colleague? A friend? Her own mother or even Maxine?* It was insane to her to imagine the number of people her father had affected, both in marvelous generosity and sinister ways. The stone they'd ordered wouldn't be delivered till early in the year. Maggie hovered at the edge of the soil so that the toes of her five-hundred-dollar boots lined the dying grass. Years ago, Maggie had once heard her father tell Alyssa that Alyssa was his favorite, if only because she had more "gumption" than Maggie. This had been ironic, as Alyssa couldn't have hated Jack Potter more.

Janine had insisted that Jack Potter loved both of his daughters equally, but only Maggie and Alyssa knew the truth of what he'd said that day. Perhaps Jack Potter would still have that power over them, if only just a little, even in death.

"Hi, Dad." Maggie pushed her hands into her coat pockets. Snow fluttered across the soil and melded with the earth. "I just found out that I can't have kids. Isn't that exciting?"

Two aisles away in the cemetery, a middle-aged woman poked her head around and gave Maggie a heinous look. Maybe it wasn't recommended to speak to the dead. Maybe there was always a fear they would talk back.

"I wonder what I would do if you were here. Would I tell you about it? Or would I let that wall between us grow thicker and thicker?" Maggie's vision shimmered with tears. She quickly swiped her glove across her cheek to catch several. "I feel somehow that my lack of ability to be a mother makes me hate you even more. Maybe because I had planned to be such a better parent than you were; maybe because I'd planned to have all this love for them that I never felt from you. But you— you got whatever you wanted and always did— at least until the end."

Maggie remained at the edge of his grave for another minute. Snow swirled around her, a constant fluffy reminder of the lateness of the year.

"But even still, Dad, I love you. And I miss you so much. Isn't that funny? Isn't it funny how you can't choose who you love? I'll laugh forever about that."

Maggie spun on her heel and headed back to the cemetery gates. Once outside, she paused before she flailed an arm out toward a passing taxi. The driver screeched the tires as he geared right-ward and allowed her entrance. Once inside, she delivered her instructions. "Brooklyn. Yours Sincerely Bar." She wanted to add, "And step on it," but in truth, traffic was wall-to-wall, with various cars weaving out in front of others suicidally as horns blared. Maggie always felt alone in the back of cabs. She could remember her very first lonely cab ride, how she had shaken so much in the back seat that her knees had clacked together. She'd heard so many stories about kidnapped teenage girls. She'd heard so many stories about city crime. When she had arrived at her destination without a problem, she'd burst into tears in disbelief. Her father had always called her "over-dramatic."

After what seemed like an hour of swirling backseat thoughts, the cab dropped Maggie off on the side of Wilson St., where she spotted Alyssa on the verge of stealing a cigarette off of one of her old high school friends Baxter. Alyssa's eyes found Maggie's as she hurried over.

"What do you think you're doing?"

Alyssa wagged her hands skyward as Maggie assessed Baxter,

who had come from privilege like Maggie and Alyssa. Unlike Maggie and Alyssa, however, Baxter liked to pretend he didn't. Maggie had heard rumors that he had taken a tiny brick-walled room with a single mattress on the floor as his current living quarters. There, he wrote poetry and pretended to live some kind of "quaint writer's life." Naturally, he would only do this until he grew tired of it when he got a huge apartment in Manhattan and worked for his father or whatever.

"Absolutely nothing, Mags," Alyssa told her.

"Really? Because it seems to me you were about to smoke."

"She's always after you, isn't she?" Baxter teased as he puffed his American Spirit.

Maggie longed to explain just how "after Alyssa" she had to be, now that she'd taken off with some Dutch guy and nearly gotten herself hurt. Now was not the time for such conversations.

The last thing she wanted was to make Alyssa feel guilty after all that. Maggie had told her, point-blank, that if she ever did something like that again, she would murder her without a second thought.

"You look weird," Alyssa told Maggie now as her brows stitched together.

Maggie shrugged. "Wow, nice to see you too, sis. I'm just cold. I'm going to head in to get a drink." She took two strides toward the door and then headed into the bar, which buzzed with early-evening conversation. A twenty-something man in an overly expensive suit flirted with a much older woman at the bar, his eyes large as he expressed to her just how much he made on Wall Street. Maggie shivered with distaste.

Then again, just how much better was Rex? He'd missed their appointment.

Maggie stepped up to the bar and ordered herself a whiskey, neat, something she had seen her father do so many times. The bartender skipped a beat to affirm her order. *Her? Whiskey?* But she stood her ground until he stepped back, grabbed the bottle, and poured her drink with a certain yet dramatic curve of his wrist. Maggie paid and glanced back through the window to catch Alyssa as she curled her hand around Baxter's elbow and cackled at something he'd said. This girl! She couldn't control herself. She was bound to make every possible mistake.

Two of Maggie and Alyssa's long-time friends lurked in the shadows of the bar. A Harvard grad named Greta drank a glass of red wine and wore a bored expression that lifted only slightly as Maggie stepped over. The other, Fred, tapped Maggie's upper back gently as a quasi-hug.

"How are you guys doing?" Maggie asked, just a split-second too late. She'd allowed the awkwardness to sink between them with her silence.

"Oh, fine. Fine," Greta replied hurriedly. "I was just telling Fred about my job interviews this week."

Maggie was half-sure she had a recent masters' degree in English Literature. Or maybe it was sculpture? Or marketing? God, her head swam horribly. She felt on the verge of either a pounding headache or a panic attack.

"And how did they go?"

"I think I'm after the office position at The Met," Greta answered. "It's a stepping-stone to other things, you know?"

"Yes. Yes, of course." Whiskey coated Maggie's tongue and made her grimace.

"And what about you? Are you still working at that gallery in Bushwick?"

Maggie wanted to laugh. It was preposterous to think of herself in any sort of field right then. Buying art for a gallery? Working in an office? Speaking with customers in any capacity? She could hardly deal with the voice in her head. Coming to this bar had been a tremendous mistake; wasn't there some sort of script to work from when it came to human interaction? Along with her faulty uterus, had she lost all human skills?

Fred tilted his head knowingly. "A lot has happened in your world lately."

"Oh, gosh. Of course." Greta sipped her wine and added, "I am so sorry about your dad. How are you holding up?"

Maggie's lips parted as she pondered what to say. Alyssa and Baxter hurried in just then, bringing a rush of chill to sweep across their cheeks. She already seemed a little tipsy, then cast herself forward as a feast of giggles erupted from her.

"Anyone need anything from the bar?" Baxter hollered.

The three of them shook their heads. A group of six cleared out from a table, allowing them to sit and wait for Alyssa and Baxter to grab another round. As they waited, another member of their Manhattan-youth arrived— Tommy, who had been living in Los Angeles for the previous eight months. Like many men of his handsomeness and bank account, he attempted to "make it big" in Hollywood.

"That's the thing about auditions. It can be a numbers game," Tommy offered as he sipped the beer Baxter had procured for him from the bar. "A few commercials here, a voice-over there... it's enough to keep anyone busy until they make it big."

"What about TV? It's impossible to pick anything to watch because there's so much. Couldn't they just insert you into one of those roles?" Alyssa giggled.

"To tell you the truth, I have a pretty big idea for a show myself," Tommy explained as his eyes sparkled. He leaned in and began to describe the plot of his TV show, which Maggie lost track of after fifteen seconds.

As Tommy continued, Baxter leaned toward Alyssa's ear and whispered something. Alyssa tossed her head back as laughter rolled over her. Baxter looked as though he'd single-handedly won World War II. He placed a hand at the small of Alyssa's back.

"But the thing about this guy's house is that it's at the edge of a crater on the moon..." Tommy said although it seemed, now, that nobody at the table listened. Even Greta picked at her nails and gazed out the window.

Alyssa pressed her lips toward Baxter's ear and whispered something. Maggie's stomach rolled with fear. When she hadn't heard from Alyssa for days after she'd taken off with that idiot Dutchman, she had thrown up due to anxiety. Bad things happened to people she loved. Despite the immensity of their trust fund, they weren't immune from heartache or death or destruction.

Alyssa seemed so cavalier about all of it. She seemed overly willing to forget that anything could go wrong at any minute. What did she care, anyway?

Minutes passed. Tommy seemed to finish his pitch for his TV show around the time Baxter professed to needing another beer. Alyssa stood with him, which allowed him to grip her tightly against him before she screeched that she needed to use the bathroom. With Alyssa gone, Maggie stood on quivering legs and headed up to the bar behind Baxter.

"You can get her taken care of first," Baxter said flirtatiously to the female bartender as Maggie eased in beside him.

The bartender rolled her eyes and turned her attention to Maggie, who ordered a shot of tequila. The woman flinched as she poured the drink without a word. Maggie dropped the shot back as Baxter whistled.

"Another, please," Maggie instructed the bartender. She no longer recognized her voice. The bartender poured her a second, which she drank immediately before turning her eyes toward Baxter's.

"You need to stay away from my sister," Maggie hissed under her breath.

"I beg your pardon?" Baxter's eyes shimmered with glee as though this was exactly how he'd hoped the evening would go. It was all a game to him.

"You heard me. Stay away from my sister."

"And what do you plan to do to keep me away from her?" Baxter demanded as he locked eyes with her.

Maggie's nostrils flared. "I will make your life a living hell. She doesn't need this right now. You're playing with fire."

"And what makes you think you know what's best in Alyssa's life?"

Alyssa's tender and beautiful face appeared between their shoulders. She giggled into a drunken "Hello!" and then lifted her lips to Baxter's cheek. Maggie stepped back, at a loss. She splayed the money she owed on the counter and ordered a glass of red wine, just something to keep her in the game. She returned to the table to pretend as though nothing had happened between her and Baxter. Once there, she found herself in another heinous conversation involving Greta articulating every modern-day artist she detested in Brooklyn. "He's arrogant and untalented, and she was born in Bangkok, so you know, uses that as her thing all the time."

Back toward the bar, Maggie watched as Baxter whispered something long-winded into Alyssa's ear. Both of their eyes found Maggie's. It was clear that Baxter told Alyssa everything that Maggie had said, with his own flourishes, of course. Maggie's cheeks burned with horror.

Alyssa disappeared for a moment. Baxter slipped back into his seat at the table and began to ask Tommy his opinion about a recent HBO show, which Tommy called "derivative." Maggie drank one-half of her wine and found her thoughts no longer connected to reality.

Maybe a minute later, maybe thirty, she felt a firm hand on her shoulder. Rex's stern face peered down at her. His scent, something so particular and uniquely his, reached her nose, despite the many strange smells within the bar. Maggie jumped up and fell into his arms as he held her. She shook uncontrollably against him as he spoke. Each syllable buzzed through his chest and then through the rest of her torso.

"I'm glad you called me," he said.

"Yeah, I have no idea what's wrong," Alyssa returned.

"I'll get her out of here. Are you good?"

"Always, Rex," Alyssa returned. "Just take care of our girl."

Maggie pulled herself around to catch Alyssa's eye. "You called him? Why?"

Alyssa's eyebrows lowered. "Let's not get into this now, Mags."

"No. Let's get into it. No time like the present."

Alyssa stiffened. "I called him because you're about to blackout and it's only seven o'clock. That's why."

Rex wrapped an arm around Maggie's stomach and lifted her away from her sister, a creature she loved with her whole heart and mind. Resentment fell over her like a shadow.

"Just be careful, Alyssa, dammit," Maggie tried, although her voice grew lost in the hubbub of the bar.

Alyssa lifted a hand to wave as Baxter rushed behind her and placed a tender, infuriating kiss across her cheek. Rex lifted Maggie's arms into her winter coat and then found her winter hat in the coat pocket. In a moment, they surged into the blistering cold, where Maggie howled with sorrow.

"Where were you today?"

Rex blinked at her with guilt-ridden eyes. He laced his hand through hers and led her to the edge of the sidewalk. Maggie was reminded of only the month before when she'd found Maxine out on her sidewalk after she had thrown a rock against Maggie's window, half-crazed in the darkness of a Brooklyn winter's night. No wonder she'd thrown the rock. No wonder she'd checked herself into an institution. Loneliness was a horror you couldn't shake. Even surrounded by some of the people she loved the most, Maggie still felt lonelier than ever. Her body had given up on her. There was no hope.

"Where were you, Rex?" she demanded again. "I called you and texted you. And I know you knew what time the appointment was. We talked about it last night and this morning."

Rex puffed out his cheeks. "You know how much pressure they're putting on me at the office. Our meeting ran long, and I couldn't just... just leave..."

A sharp wind rushed between them and caught Rex's scarf so that it whirled up and away from him. He reached out to grab it just in the nick of time.

"It was important, Rex," Maggie blared.

"But you're young, Maggie. We're both young. We have so much time to keep trying," Rex returned.

"So you're saying it wasn't important enough for you to leave your meeting?" Maggie demanded.

Rex re-wrapped his scarf hurriedly, exasperated. "Tell me, then. What happened?"

Maggie's lips parted with sorrow. She blinked up at this man, whom she'd pledged to love her entire life. Rex lifted an arm to grab a taxi as another wind surged between them.

"It was fine. They said it was all fine," Maggie snapped back, just as a taxi rushed to the side, a wave of bright yellow.

Rex studied her face for a moment. The corners of his lips curved slightly upward. *Why had she lied to him? Why had the truth seemed like such an impossibility? What was wrong with her?*

"That's great, Maggie. That's really great. I guess we'll just keep trying, right? One of my favorite things to do, anyway." He kissed her gently and then eased the back of the taxi open to allow her first entrance. He slid in after her and told the cab driver their address before bringing his muscular arm around her and holding her close.

As the taxi driver sped them back toward the apartment they'd shared for years, Maggie's soul dug itself deeper into the darkness. When she lifted her eyes to Rex, she only saw a stranger, not the man she thought she knew.

Chapter Four

The woman who had agreed to sublease Linda's rent-controlled apartment for the month of December (and potentially beyond) expressed such excitement at the price. She was in her late twenties and on the verge of "making it" on Broadway. She could just feel it. As she buzzed through Linda's apartment, she brought with her a wave of what seemed to be heinously expensive perfume— the likes of which Linda had only smelled on the super-rich ladies who'd shopped at DENISE. Linda was grateful to the woman for taking the apartment. Together with this month's rent and the small amount of savings she had in her bank account, Linda was armed and ready for her trek. She hadn't been outside of the city in years— and hardly off of Manhattan. It had the potential to be the adventure of a lifetime (or the worst mistake).

Before she departed from the city, Linda stopped at a little magazine stand and purchased the gossip magazine that held the story of Janine Potter and Maxine Aubert. At Port Authority Bus

Station, she pored over the glossy pages and assessed the tiny photographs of Maxine and Janine as they bustled through the streets of Edgartown. In Linda's mind, Edgartown had become the quintessential locale for Christmas— none of the smog of the city. All of the bright and glittering Christmas lights and cozy cafés and bustling Christmas shoppers, but none of the loneliness of New York City.

Besides, without a job, how was she meant to spend her days?

She needed a place to go... a place to feel focused. A place to dig deeper into herself and feel, well, like the woman she'd been before. She supposed that woman still lurked within her, somewhere. At sixty-five, this was perhaps her last shot at making contact.

The bus trip from New York City to Woods Hole, Massachusetts, was said to take six hours and forty-five minutes. When the bus arrived, just before ten in the morning, Linda received another text from her sub-leaser, gushing about how close the apartment was to her boyfriend (who also worked on Broadway, she'd been careful to point out). Linda's stomach felt hollow and cold. It seemed already that her sub-leaser belonged in her apartment far more than she did.

Was there anywhere on this earth she belonged?

The bus was only half-filled. It was a Monday, which made a trek from the city to Martha's Vineyard more unlikely. Linda removed her shoes and spread her legs out on the seat beside her. The magazine remained partly opened on an article about the importance of moisturizing your face with retinol. Linda snatched a hand mirror from her purse and inspected her reflection. Although she'd never had the money for expensive surgery, botox, or even the finer "creams," she'd aged rather gracefully. Wrinkles were mere whispers across her forehead and around her eyes. She attributed this to her previous few decades of sunscreen. Besides that, she had never smoked, not even when it was a rather common activity across many of her strange locales, including Europe and Asia.

When the bus arrived in Woods Hole, Linda stepped out on creaking legs and found herself on a strange island. It was mid-afternoon, closing in on evening, but the air remained chilly and bright, the sky cloudless and almost sinister in the density of its blue. Linda had packed only a backpack, which she now swung over her shoulder as she directed herself toward the ferry docks. As it was December, the schedule was limited, but the internet had told her there would be another ferry to Oak Bluffs at six p.m., which was just a few minutes away.

Much like the bus before it, the ferry itself was half-empty, with travelers ducking into the belly of the boat to buy cups of hot coffee and cozy up together, an escape from the howling ocean winds. By contrast, Linda was mesmerized by the rollicking waves as they surged against the ferry boat. She hovered at the edge, her hands gripping the railing, and blinked out toward the horizon line as they headed toward that glorious rock in the Atlantic, tucked between the Nantucket and Vineyard Sounds.

"First time?" The voice rang out from just left of her and very nearly grew lost in the whistling winds.

Linda blinked over to find a rugged-looking man in his mid to late sixties, with broad, muscular shoulders. He wore a ferry captain's uniform and an overly-thick beard, and his seafoam eyes danced with the Massachusetts sunlight.

"First time on the island?" he asked again, assuming she hadn't heard.

"Yes, it is," Linda replied hurriedly. She slipped a strand of hair behind her ear and tried on a smile.

"I can tell. You've got that look to you."

Linda arched an eyebrow. "What look would that be?"

"Like you're on an adventure," he articulated back.

Linda's smile strengthened.

"Where are you staying?"

"The Katama Lodge," she answered.

"Ah. Great place." His eyes grew shadowed for a moment. "My dear old friend owned and operated it since it opened its doors many years ago. It was his life and his love. Neal Remington. He passed away just last January. It broke the island's heart."

Always when someone expressed sorrow over a death, Linda's heart ached with fear that nobody would remember her when she passed on. No one would think of her at all. It was a selfish thought, but it held the weight of truth.

"I'm terribly sorry to hear that," Linda told him, just loud enough to be heard over the rush of the winds.

"But the Lodge, it's a treasure of a place," the captain continued. "Brings women in from all over the world. These days, Neal's wife, Nancy, runs the place with her stepdaughters and daughter, Janine. Great women all-around. Janine works as the head doctor, I believe, and the others do their part in other fields. Acupuncture and the like. I, for one, can't imagine getting pinged with so many needles at once..."

Linda grimaced. She had read about acupuncture online but had already ruled it out for herself. "It seems unnatural, doesn't it?"

"My thoughts exactly."

Linda giggled as bubbles of excitement overtook her stomach.

"I don't know what to expect from any of it. I just left the city after years of feeling trapped inside."

"Years in the city? You couldn't pay me enough to do that. I need all this water. I need all this sun. I need the freedom of nature," the captain told her.

Linda hadn't spoken to a stranger like this in decades. She had already told more to this man than she had to Connie, who she'd worked alongside for a number of months. Linda had never bothered to tell Connie her specific coffee order for fear that Connie would forget it. This forgetfulness would serve as a reminder of just how little anyone cared for Linda. She knew those thoughts were ridiculous, but she couldn't help herself.

The captain started to walk back to the control station but beckoned for Linda to follow him and hover in the doorway. As he steered, he pointed toward her backpack and said, "That doesn't look like anything a woman meant for the Lodge would carry. Normally, they bring about five suitcases, with three different dinner outfit options per night."

Linda had hardly packed enough for a couple of days, let alone the two weeks she had booked at the Lodge.

"I hope they won't kick me out for being not-as-fashion-forward," Linda joked.

"I'm sure you'll be fine. It'll probably give you more focus, you know. On whatever it is you're going to the Lodge for." He cleared his throat as the motor sputtered strangely beneath them. "My wife— she's long gone now... cancer, but she used to head off to the Lodge every time her stress levels got too bad. Neal always gave her a deal. She came back home all bright and shiny and alive. I was jealous. It seemed to me that Neal should have started some kind of spa for men. I guess that's what fishing is for us, huh?"

KATIE WINTERS

"I suppose so," Linda tried.

"What about you?"

Linda's throat tightened. "What do you mean, what about me?"

"I mean, was there anyone?"

Linda hadn't told a single soul this information in multiple decades. Yet here it was, the truth. What did she have to lose?

"I was married for a while. It didn't work out."

He nodded as his eyes grew shadowed. What was worse, losing your love to cancer or losing your love to the idiocy of early adulthood? Linda wasn't sure. Regardless, they'd both loved and lost, as had so many others of their age. She stirred in silence for a long moment as the waves gushed across the hull.

To the left of the steering wheel, the captain had positioned a name tag, presumably something he was meant to wear at all times. She pointed at it and asked, "Joshua?"

"That's the name," he affirmed. "But I hate the name tag. I can't tell you how many times tourists have gotten up in my face and said, 'Thank you, Joshua,' just as proof that they saw the thing. I don't like people up in my face. I need space!"

Linda chuckled. She couldn't remember the last time anyone had been closer to her than a full foot away. "They must be amazed at your life as a captain on the Sound."

"Men always like to ask me how it works, how I got into this line of work. The truth is, I'm an islander, just like my dad and my granddad and my great-granddad before me. My dad and grandfather both drove the ferries for this very line."

"Nepotism?" Linda teased.

"Something like that. Rather, our little island is insular. People come for the summer, but they make sure to escape at the first sign of a chill in the air. We islanders stick around for the long haul."

"So you're saying the people who ask you how you became a captain just couldn't understand?"

"Nobody can understand the Vineyard fully without spending some years on it, I reckon," Joshua continued. "I feel more at-home on the water than I do in my house. Back and forth, back and forth. It's how I spend my days. But I can't complain. You see some of the most beautiful sunrises and sunsets. You feel a part of the winds and the rain. And you see people like you, on the verge of adventure. It's all pretty magical."

Linda blushed again, just as Joshua lifted a hand to point out the incoming Oak Bluffs ferry docks. He focused up and eased the boat toward the little collection of colonial-looking houses that curved around the Oak Bluffs Marina. Linda gripped the edge of the doorway as they trekked forward. Down below, one of the ferry dock workers onboard flung a rope to a dock worker, who tied them up with a succinct and experienced whip of his wrist.

"Guess this is your stop," Joshua said as he cut the engine.

Linda met his gaze as her heart thumped. This was the first man she'd had a full conversation with in perhaps ten years. *How had she done it with such ease?*

"Thank you for bringing us in safely," she told him with a quick nod of her head. "I've loved every minute of this time out at sea. You live a beautiful life."

Before he could say another word, Linda slipped her backpack across her shoulders and scuttled back down the steps. Downstairs, the dockworker lined the ramp from the boat to dock up to allow for the travelers to dismount, one after another. She breezed past a couple of sixty-somethings as though she was two decades

41

younger than them. Perhaps it was the possibility of a possibility that put such lightness to her steps. Perhaps it was this feeling that all would soon be okay, if only she believed in it.

When Linda stepped off the dock, she found herself face-to-face with a twenty-something woman who held a sign that read: LINDA. Linda's heart jumped into her throat. It was just like what you saw in the movies. Linda waved a hand as the young woman waved back and allowed the sign to fall to her side.

"Hello." Linda greeted the young girl and assessed her with her dark blue eyes and dark long brown hair, which cascaded across her shoulders and down her back. Her large black coat seemed overly large for her, dwarfing her small frame.

"Hi, welcome to Martha's Vineyard. I'm Mallory. They had me come pick you up since our normal van driver is off today."

Linda adjusted her backpack, which had begun to strain her spine. Mallory hurried around to help the backpack off her back.

"You shouldn't have to carry your luggage," Mallory insisted.

"Oh honey, that's okay. I'm used to carrying my stuff around."

Mallory's smile brightened. "Don't worry. My baby's about a year and a half these days. Your backpack weighs just about the same as he does. I'm used to lugging him around."

Mallory led Linda to the company van, on which the words KATAMA LODGE AND WELLNESS SPA had been scribed. She sat in the back, feeling like a fool while this young woman sped her south and east to the far end of the island.

"Did you grow up on the island?" Linda heard herself ask.

"I did! My mother and father were islanders, as was my grandfather. My grandfather owned the Lodge."

"Ah. Your grandfather must have been Neal."

"Yes. He was a very special man," Mallory murmured. "I miss

him every day. I sometimes think, when times get especially tough, I would love to speak to him. Ask his advice. It feels like I lost this vessel of wisdom when he left the world..."

Linda's energy shifted lower. She dropped her head back on the headrest as the snow-capped houses and trees sped past on either side. Regardless of where you were or who you spoke with, it seemed every piece of humanity was touched with loss.

"Here we are..." Mallory announced their arrival as they made their way down a long, curving road, which eased them toward a miraculous-looking cabin at the edge of a multi-acreage property alongside the beach and multiple hiking trails. "My grandfather's house is further west of here, on one hundred acres. We recently moved in there all together. Me, my mother, my baby... and so many others. It's one big happy house of many, many women, kind of like our own personal Katama Lodge."

Linda wasn't sure how to respond to this. She wondered if Janine Potter was amongst them, as it seemed she was the daughter of Neal Remington's widow.

"Let me grab your backpack from the back. You must be very tired from your journey." Mallory hopped out and walked around to the trunk as Linda stepped onto the driveway. Winter chill swept over her and caused her eyes to become glassy. In the far distance, several women walked along the waterline, all bundled up in winter coats as the ocean frothed across a frigid beach.

Was this where everything would come together? Was this where Linda's life would begin again?

Once inside, Mallory hustled around to her seat at the front desk and pulled out an itinerary for the first few days of Linda's stay. Linda gripped the handle of her backpack as Malloy instructed Linda on the next two days.

"You're here just in time for dinner. Normally, we focus here on nutritionally vibrant meals, often vegan. We have a world-renowned chef who's skilled in fixing your body's internal composition and maximizing health." Mallory lowered her voice to add, "I've never felt better than I have since I started working here. She helped me drop the baby weight and decreased my anxiety, I swear. Food is terribly important. I don't think I understood that before."

Linda thought back to her many, many years of eating nothing but Cream of Wheat. What had that done to her body? What had that singular, depressing act done to her mind?

"Hi there." A beautiful and athletic woman of five foot five stepped out from the nearest office. She wore a black blazer and a neutral lip color and lifted a hand in greeting to Linda. "You must be Linda. I'm Elsa, director of public relations and events here at the Lodge."

"That's my mom," Mallory explained. "She's in charge of just about everything around here, to be honest with you."

Linda greeted Elsa warmly. There was kindness behind the woman's eyes that seemed unmatched in any other woman across Manhattan. Linda's stomach loosened slightly. Perhaps she would be safe there. Perhaps she wouldn't have to be alone, at least for a while.

Chapter Five

"You have to hear this song." Alyssa turned up the volume as she surged down the highway in their mother's vehicle, which she had borrowed to visit the city. It was a recent hip-hop track, nothing Maggie had ever heard of. It penetrated straight through her eardrums like needles. As Alyssa bopped around behind the wheel, Maggie turned down the volume. Alyssa shrieked, "Hey! We haven't even gotten to the good part."

"I can still hear it," Maggie pointed out, disgruntled.

Silence brewed between them. Alyssa snapped off the radio and gave Maggie a sidelong glance. "What the heck has gotten into you, Mags?"

Maggie glared out the window. They had left the city a little more than an hour ago and were somewhere on I-95 in Connecticut, mere miles from the water's edge. Sometime around three in the morning, as Rex's snores had escalated in volume, Maggie had reached for her phone and asked Alyssa if she could tag along back to the island. Alyssa, being Alyssa, had still been at one bar or another and texted back a resounding "YES!"

"You were so weird yesterday," Alyssa pointed out finally. "Is everything okay?"

Maggie shrugged flippantly and turned back on the radio full-blast. Alyssa sputtered back into the song and bopped around. All had been forgotten, at least for the moment.

When Maggie had announced to Rex that she planned to go to the island for "a week, maybe more," he'd stopped mid-way through tying his tie and given her a blank expression. His tie fell flat on both sides of his neck.

"Is this about the doctor's appointment? Because I promise you that I won't miss any others. I just really couldn't leave yesterday. It was a, 'Do I want to get fired today or not?' situation."

Maggie had shaken her head sadly, her feet flat on the floor beside their bed as she gazed toward the grey light that swept in through the window. She was a city girl, just like her mother and grandmother before her. But her mother and grandmother had found fresh air and new life on the Vineyard. It was therapeutic. Maggie needed healing just then, especially after the heart-wrenching news the doctor had given her.

"I'm homesick. I just miss Mom," Maggie had explained softly. "We've had a really strange year. I want as much time with her as I can get."

Rex had positioned himself next to her on the bed and spread a hand over her upper back. Maggie had sensed that he'd wanted to make love then. She had stood instead and reached for her suitcase.

"We can keep trying when you're back," Rex had said after a moment's pause. He'd then returned to his tie, which he latched up safely against his neck with the promptness of a businessman who had places to be.

Would he become Jack Potter one day? Maggie shuddered again at the thought.

"Want to grab something to eat?" Alyssa asked, pulling Maggie from her thoughts. They passed by a selection of fast food joints.

Maggie grumbled inwardly. Food was the furthest thing from her mind.

"I'm hungover and making an executive decision," Alyssa countered as she slipped the car into the exit lane and headed for the nearest Burger King. As they hovered in the take-out lane, Alyssa rubbed her eyes so roughly that her fingers drew back black eye makeup. "Shoot."

Maggie's stomach gurgled with hunger.

"What do you want?" Alyssa demanded.

"Absolutely nothing." Maggie hadn't eaten a single portion of fast food since her college years.

"Don't be dumb. I can hear your stomach from all the way over here."

Maggie rolled her eyes. "I don't want anything."

Alyssa heaved a sigh. The cars shifted forward to put them closer to the radio, where she would assuredly order her normal BK order of a Junior Whopper with fries and a strawberry milkshake. Maggie had seen her drag herself through a hangover just this way countless times.

"I didn't sleep with him, by the way," Alyssa blurted out suddenly.

Maggie arched an eyebrow. She wasn't sure what to say. Disappointment in herself merged with embarrassment, and she dropped her eyes to her hands, which were chapped from the winter chill.

"I would have, probably," Alyssa continued.

Maggie gave her sister a sideway glance just then. "I didn't mean to ruin your evening."

"No. It's really for the best. Baxter and I are better as friends. And if I had, well. I would probably be going through a whole lot of self-hatred right now. So, I guess I owe you a thank you."

Their car reached the speaker. Alyssa drew open the window to bring in a gust of horrific New England winter. The man behind the radio asked her what she wanted, and Alyssa ordered a Junior Whopper, fries, a strawberry milkshake, "And...um... a spicy chicken sandwich with onion rings. And a chocolate shake."

"Alyssa! I don't want anything."

"That'll be thirteen forty-seven," the man behind the radio blared.

"Thank you!" Alyssa gave Maggie a mischievous glance before she drove up to allow the car behind them to snake in behind.

"I didn't want anything," Maggie repeated. "And I don't even know if their chicken sandwiches are good."

Alyssa shrugged. "They're delicious. Everything here is made of gold. And whatever's bugging you? It'll put it to rest for at least an hour. Maybe three, depending on how much you like onion rings."

A few minutes later, Alyssa parked the car near Plum Bank Marsh Wildlife Area, with a beautiful view of the Back River. She rustled through the paper bags and handed a chicken burger and a container of onion rings over to Maggie.

Was this the right time to tell Alyssa what was really on her mind?

Or was it better to shove the thoughts away?

"Look, I get it." Alyssa took a bite of her fry and chewed thoughtfully. "Dad's been on my mind, too. I can't make peace with a lot of it. Some of the cruel things he said to me remain in the back of my mind. Maybe they'll be there forever."

Maggie ate one-half of an onion ring and watched as a large, fat-bellied red cardinal stepped lightly upon a branch just above them.

"I think it's just going to take some time," she continued.

During the previous few months, especially, Maggie had avoided non-traditional food, candy, and drank less and less, all to create a beautiful and healthy environment for her potential baby. With the first sinful bite of her chicken sandwich, she nearly moaned with pleasure. How awful it was to treat your body like garbage. But maybe it was appropriate when your body treated you like garbage right back.

"It's incredible," Alyssa affirmed as she wrapped up her trash a few minutes later. "It's the perfect hangover remedy. I feel like I could run twelve miles right now."

"Okay, go for it. I'll wait in the car," Maggie countered with a lopsided grin.

"Funny girl."

Several hours later, Maggie and Alyssa arrived back at the house on the southern edge of the island to find Nancy in the midst of what could only be called a "Christmas Fit." She hovered over several boxes of decorations with a manic expression across her face. With a jolt, Maggie realized: this was Nancy's first Christmas without

49

Neal. It was her first Christmas as a widow. It was also the first Christmas she would spend with her daughter and granddaughters ever.

"Grandma! What are you up to?" Alyssa asked as she stepped around the boxes and into her grandmother's arms.

"Look at you! I didn't expect both of you back today." Grandma Nancy hurried around to catch Maggie and Alyssa both in her arms. "And I certainly didn't expect you to reek of fast food. Where have you been?"

"Come on, Grandma. You can't knock fast food," Alyssa replied. "It's there for you when you need it."

"I suppose I've had my fair share," Nancy agreed. "Let me get you, girls, some mulled wine. And then, dare I ask that you help me set up for Christmas? It's already the sixth, for goodness sakes, and I want us all to enjoy them. Our house is full! And we've even got little ones coming in and out. I want it to be magical."

Maggie's stomach tightened with sorrow. Little ones! Cody's daughter, Gretchen, and Mallory's baby, Zachery, had filled her with light over the previous few months. She had felt her love for them like a prophecy. She was meant to be a mother.

Grandma Nancy poured them each a glass of hot mulled wine and then pressed upon them the importance of each strand of garland and each piece of tinsel. "The Holy Night Scene needs to be put up near the door, and goodness, we have to replace nearly all of the photographs with these framed Christmas ones. Oh, look at Neal, Elsa, and Carmella in this one! Poor Carmella looks so unhappy in her elf costume."

"She looks on the verge of attacking the other two," Alyssa affirmed.

Maggie found herself at the Christmas tree, a good place to

zone out and position large bulbs from Christmas's past in well-thought-out locations. She hadn't yet put up her and Rex's tree and now shivered at the thought. How could she possibly return as though everything hadn't changed and make their house all Christmas-y and warm?

Alyssa set up a portable speaker and played Christmas tunes, Nat King Cole, Mariah Carey, and Bing Crosby. Grandma Nancy alternated between giving instructions to Alyssa and Maggie and singing along with the speaker. Alyssa went to and fro, from the mulled wine which remained warm in the crock pot, to the Christmas tree and back again.

"I'll keep us well-stocked," she informed Maggie under her breath.

"Oh good," Grandma Nancy greeted Carmella as she entered. "We need so much help!"

Carmella laughed brightly and hugged her stepmother warmly. The wave of her left hand flashed with her new engagement ring. "What can I do?"

When the tree was finished, Maggie headed into the kitchen to see what to do about dinner. Very soon, her mother, Elsa, Mallory, and perhaps others, including Elsa's boyfriend, Bruce, or Carmella's fiancé, Cody, or even Cole, Elsa's son, might arrive for dinner, and it was better to have a large portion ready. Leftovers were key in that house, as anyone could be hungry at any time. There, in the midst of the hustle and bustle of the gorgeous house at the edge of the island, Maggie was allowed the freedom to forget.

Maggie sliced onions and peppers on a quest to make soul-warming chili with fresh cornbread. Alyssa weaved in and out, helped for brief moments at a time, then scrambled back out to Grandma Nancy to chat about whatever else came to her mind.

Maggie again cursed herself for her lack of "free-spiritedness," which Alyssa had in spades. Again, her father's voice rang through her mind. Alyssa was it for him. Not Maggie.

A few minutes later, there was a dark and brooding voice in the foyer. Maggie stopped slicing to listen more intently.

"She isn't back from work yet." This was Grandma Nancy, whose tone had lost its warmth.

"She told me she'd be back by now."

"I don't know what to tell you. Sometimes, things get busy up there. Have you texted her?"

"No. I just planned to drop the baby off right now. I have plans."

Maggie placed her knife on the counter and wiped her hands on a nearby towel. As she entered the living area, baby Zachery let out an excruciating wail. His father, Lucas, was the one who now held him. His face twisted with disgust at Zachery's noises.

"What's the matter?" Maggie asked in a sharp tone.

Lucas adjusted baby Zachery against his chest. Nancy flung up her hands and said, "Have a seat, Lucas. She'll be home soon."

"This wasn't the agreement. I have plans."

Nancy stalked off, clearly annoyed. Alyssa turned to grab a Christmas cookie, which she nibbled as she turned away from him. This left Maggie and Lucas in a sort of face-off as Zachery's wails quieted.

"I can't stay," Lucas told her pointedly.

"You know what? I don't like your tone," Maggie returned.

"This doesn't concern you."

"It does," Maggie blared. "Mallory is my cousin."

"Step-cousin."

"You're unbelievable. Thanks for the correction. Anyway.

What's your plan now? You're going to belittle Mallory for being late when you know very well she takes her job seriously? You're going to just drop off Zachery and head off to wherever the heck you had plans? You know that your family should be your first priority, right?"

Obviously, this all came from a very dark place— one that had very little to do with Lucas. Still, the words were there, and they spilled out like water from a hose.

"I just don't understand men like you," Maggie continued. "You think your world is the first priority, and everything else comes second or third or fourth. It disgusts me."

Maggie then flung herself forward, took baby Zachery from Lucas's arms, and shot up the staircase. "Leave his stuff at the door!" she hollered.

The quick movements made Zachery shriek, but the shriek was filled with joy and excitement. It was the same sound he made when one of them tossed him into the air and caught him again. What a marvelous baby he was. How was it possible that Lucas could look at this baby with anything but complete love and adoration?

Didn't people understand what a gift it was to bring a baby into this world?

When Maggie reached the bedroom, the one she and Alyssa had shared for the previous six months or so, she and Zachery huddled together on the bed and fell into a much-needed sleep. Outside, the clouds stitched together to form the perfect, dark-colored quilt, one that cast another layer of fluffy snow across the island. Maggie did not dream.

Chapter Six

The creak of the door felt from another world. With the curtains drawn tight over the windows, Maggie and Alyssa's room was dark as a tomb. Beside Maggie, Zachery stirred only slightly, straightening his chubby little leg all the way out. He was akin to a little heater; the air around him was milky, soft, and warm. Maggie blinked her eyes wider as a sliver of light widened over the bed. Someone had come into the room.

"Maggie?" Her mother's voice was sweet and lilting. "Are you awake?"

Maggie turned slightly and lifted her back up onto her pillow. Her mother leaned against the doorway and folded her arms over her chest. Maggie could sense the fear in her mother's eyes. Only a few weeks ago, she'd had to spin all her worries for Alyssa's disappearance. Now, her other daughter acted irrationally. Probably, she didn't have the mental strength to handle it.

"I'm up."

Janine tip-toed to the edge of the bed. Her weight dimpled the mattress only slightly as she slid a hand over Maggie's shoulder. Worry permeated her face.

"What happened, honey? They said you had words with Lucas."

Maggie groaned inwardly. Baby Zachery buzzed his lips through his sleep.

"You know I've never really liked Lucas," Maggie responded simply.

Janine laughed lightly. "Nobody does, do they? Not good enough for our Mallory."

"It's more than that, Mom," Maggie told her. She placed a hand tenderly over her stomach and felt the hollowness of her insides. "I just can't understand..." But she trailed off. It was increasingly clear to her just how alienated she felt and how little her outburst had to do with Lucas's treatment of Mallory and Zachery. She forced her eyes toward her mother's and tried out a smile. "I just want the best for them. And besides, I was exhausted. I needed a nap more than Zach did."

"I didn't expect you today. Alyssa said it was a surprise for her, too."

"There's not a lot going on in the city," Maggie tried, although her mother knew good-and-well how fat of a lie that was. "And besides, I'm about to have a few job interviews. This could be my last chance for a spontaneous trek to the island."

Janine's eyes attempted to dig into Maggie's, but she dropped her gaze back to Zachery in avoidance.

"Mallory's here. I think she wants Zach up for a few hours before putting him to bed," Janine murmured. "Just so he sleeps through the night."

Sleep schedules. Food schedules. Playtime schedules.

Doctor's appointments. Future preschools and kindergartens. Parents found themselves faced with seemingly countless conundrums and decisions as their baby morphed from being such a tiny creature to a long-legged, chubby-cheeked child. Maggie longed for those decisions. She longed to rant at Rex about her lack of sleep. She longed to find spit-up on her blouse and laugh at it.

Maggie lifted Zachery's toasty little body and carried him into the hallway. The hall mirror reflected a mussed-hair, creased-cheek version of Maggie. Janine, too, chuckled at this version of her. She patted Maggie's curls to try to tame them. Zach clutched Maggie's sweater with tremendous force as he awakened bit-by-bit.

The living room looked like a Christmas explosion. Mallory jumped up from the couch with her arms outstretched as baby Zachery cooed with delight.

"There he is! My handsome man." She locked eyes with Maggie and added, "Thank you for taking him for a while after Lucas..."

"Don't worry about it," Maggie told her.

"It was really my fault. I told him I'd be here in time."

Maggie's stomach sizzled with acid. Mallory turned with baby Zachery and then perched alongside Elsa, who wagged a hand at Zachery in greeting. The joy that permeated across Elsa's face sliced through Maggie like a knife. Janine deserved that kind of happiness.

Like a lost pup, Maggie walked into the kitchen after Janine to find Alyssa and Grandma Nancy mid-way through a joint cooking-plus-yoga session. The large pot of chili bubbled on the stovetop as Nancy and Alyssa arched their spines into Downward Dog.

"Burger King plus yoga? Alyssa, you live a varied life," Maggie tried out a joke.

"Life is about balance, sis," Alyssa replied to the floor.

Janine poured the four of them glasses of wine. A bag of sweet potato chips was open on the table, and she selected a small slab and placed it on her tongue. Grandma Nancy slowly crept back to standing and then stepped over to hug Maggie. "You know, honey, it's very sweet what you did for Zachery today."

Would this ever stop being the topic at hand? Maggie's cheeks burned with embarrassment. She sipped her wine and grimaced as Carmella entered to check on the cornbread, which she'd taken over when Maggie had raced upstairs with baby Zachery.

"And how long are you staying with us this time?" Grandma Nancy asked Maggie brightly, as a way to bridge them through the awkward silence.

"I'm not sure," Maggie told her.

"And Rex is okay with that?" Grandma Nancy asked with a subtle arch of her eyebrow.

"Yes, of course. Rex knows he's got a free spirit on his hands," Alyssa countered as she crunched through several sweet potato chips.

"Funny." Maggie rolled her eyes. "Rex has a lot going on right now with work."

Janine's eyes darkened for a split second. Was it recognition? Could she, too, see Jack Potter in Rex's maneuvers? Did it frighten her?

"It's good that he'll get this all done before Christmas," Grandma Nancy tried. "That way, we can all relax here on the Vineyard together."

As conversation found its way to other topics, Maggie headed

58

for the dining room to set the table. Janine was hot on her heels, her arms heavy with crystal water glasses. As Maggie placed a plate delicately before each chair, Janine's eyes burned toward her. After a long pause, Janine murmured, "You'd tell me if something was wrong between you and Rex, wouldn't you?"

Maggie felt a resounding *NO* within her.

Here, a lie was the better route.

"Of course."

Janine's face relaxed slightly. She added several crystal glasses around the table. Each caught the splendorous light from the hanging dining room light and sparkled strange designs across the walls. Maggie tried to force her mind to churn outwards. There was a real obsession about her just then. She couldn't see the world from any other perspective.

"How was work today?" Maggie finally asked.

Janine's voice brightened. "Really good. The Lodge is completely booked, as usual, and my appointment schedule seems heavier than ever."

"And Maxine? Is she still at the Lodge?"

Janine shook her head. "She's moved to a little rental apartment in downtown Edgartown. It's a quaint little place, fully decorated by someone who Maxine calls 'tasteless.'"

"Ooph. It sounds like a pretty big insult, coming from Maxine."

"Maxine is accustomed to Manhattan chic," Janine affirmed.

"Do you think she'll head back to the city any time soon?"

"I've asked her," Janine replied delicately. "But honestly, she doesn't have many people there. I'm her family— for better or for worse."

Maggie's stomach curdled against this news. Although she'd

loved Maxine like an aunt her entire life, the hatred she had brewed against her after her affair with Jack Potter was difficult to deconstruct. Her mother's ability to forgive seemed otherworldly.

"Anyway, she wants to look at houses," Janine continued as she steadied the final crystal glass in place. "Here on the island."

"Oh. Wow." This was a level of permanence Maggie hadn't counted on.

"We're going tomorrow if you'd like to join us," Janine offered. "If you're not committed to anything else."

Maggie smeared her hand over her lips. *What the heck else would she do?* "That sounds pretty good."

"We'd love your artistic eye," Janine affirmed brightly. "And you know how Maxine feels about you."

Yep. Maggie knew. Maggie had gotten the hint when Maxine had traveled to Brooklyn last month to throw pebbles at her window. Love made people do insane things.

A rap at the door drew Henry, Janine's newly official boyfriend, into their midst. He carried flowers and placed a kiss on Janine's cheek as she blushed. It had been difficult for Janine to accept the love Henry wanted to give her. Henry had even bailed on his commitment to a documentary project in China, something that would take him from the island (and away from Janine) for up to a year. They had both decided on one another. Amid the mess of their existence, they'd committed to making things work.

"Let's eat, shall we?" Grandma Nancy hollered from the kitchen. "Alyssa says she's starving."

"Grandma..." Alyssa teased. "Don't give me away."

Together, the hodgepodge family of the Potters, the Grimsons, and Remingtons gathered around the table for yet another wonderful home-cooked meal. It was easy to fall into the rhythm of the conversation. It reminded Maggie of a song. She positioned her spoon beneath the goopy chili beans and forgot to eat. Janine had told her that when she'd first learned she was pregnant with Maggie, she hadn't known how to tell Jack Potter, as she'd been frightened he would deal with it all wrong. "He surprised me. He surprised me with his love. I don't think I'll ever forget that," Janine had told her.

Her chili untouched, Maggie erupted from the table and headed for the living room. Silence stretched out behind her.

"Honey? You okay?" Janine called.

"Yep!" Maggie called back without lending any additional context. She rushed to the bathroom, where she clicked the door closed and gripped either side of the sink. The eyes in her reflection in the mirror told her to pull it together. But every act of normalcy seemed a reminder of the secret she now held close to her heart. She felt so wrong, like poison permeating through everything.

Chapter Seven

On Linda's second morning at the Katama Lodge and Wellness Spa, she awoke just past five and tip-toed her way to the small window to peer out across Katama Bay. Hers was the smallest of the available Lodge rooms, with a window the size of an A4 piece of paper. Even still, the soft glow of approaching dawn eased through the glass and lifted her spirits. Every moment away from Manhattan seemed to lift her spirits. Her skin seemed smoother, her joints looser. When she asked her mind to replay images of DENISE or her rent-controlled apartment, she struggled with accuracy. She seemed eternally focused in the present, for once.

Nancy Remington's six a.m. yoga session had been far down on Linda's list of to-dos. Yoga seemed a trend for the "younger generation," something that would make her already-aching back ache more. But now, she found herself slipping into a pair of leggings and a light t-shirt and heading into the hallway, on the hunt for this apparently "soul-healing" extravaganza. She'd already come all the way to the Vineyard. She might as well lean into life at the Lodge.

The other women lined up outside the yoga studio were in their twenties, thirties, and forties. Linda felt bland and tired-looking when compared to them. A woman in her forties greeted her with a soft, "Good morning!" Linda forced a smile in return. As she attempted to drum up some kind of response, Nancy drew open the door and beckoned them to enter. A soft drum beat welcomed them from the hanging speakers. Nancy instructed them each to take a yoga mat and line them up in three rows.

"We have a small group this morning," she breathed. "Which I have to admit, I prefer."

As Linda splayed her yoga mat across the hardwood floor, she glanced up to find Nancy smiling down at her curiously. Linda's heart quickened. The last thing she wanted was special treatment due to her age. Nancy spread her arms wide and returned her gaze just above the heads of the group. "We'll begin today with child's pose," she said sweetly as she aligned herself on her yoga mat. "It's a beautiful way to get the breath going before we continue with the rest of the exercises. Breath always comes first."

Linda curled into a child's pose and focused on her breathing, something she wasn't sure she'd done in many years, perhaps ever. As her lungs filled, her anxious thoughts slowed remarkably. She closed her eyes and eased into the comfort of her body. Was this how other people felt all the time? Had she assumed her car crash of a mind was the standard?

The yoga session lasted forty-five minutes. Linda couldn't quite reach many of the poses, but she pushed herself and found a strength within her limbs and core she hadn't expected. When they ended at the child's pose again, she inhaled and exhaled along with the rest of the group. It was as though they all breathed as one.

After Nancy released them, the other women (or, in Linda's mind, "girls") packed up their things, spoke lightly with one another and prepared to head off to breakfast. Linda felt languid and slow. She returned her yoga mat and walked toward the door, where Nancy said goodbye to everyone with warm, soft tones. Linda was the last to leave. She again locked eyes with Nancy, who cocked her head and said, "It's so good to see someone my age around here."

Linda stopped short, surprised at Nancy's frankness. Nancy's eyes were a comfort to gaze into. She had to say something back— something that mattered. But what?

"It was my first yoga session."

"And how did you like it?" Nancy asked.

"Oh, it was just so different than I imagined." Linda was surprised at her answer yet grateful for her honesty.

Nancy's grin widened. "I thought the same thing when I got into it. It was a later-in-life thing for me. I spent the first thirty-plus years of my life a shell of myself. I don't think I had a sip of water till thirty-five."

Linda laughed appreciatively. "I suppose it's good to know you can start whenever you want at this whole personal wellness thing."

"It's never too late. And it's always necessary to focus on yourself for a change. I imagine you've spent most of your life focused on just about everyone else but yourself."

Linda had no idea how to respond to this. She kept her lips pressed tightly shut.

"Where are you from?" Nancy asked after a moment of

silence.

"The city. I mean, New York. Sorry. It's just, to me..."

"The only place that could ever be called a city? I know. Me too. I grew up there and raised my daughter there," Nancy confirmed. "And gosh, it's changed over the years since I left."

"It really has," Linda offered sadly. "Not my same Manhattan."

"I was a Brooklyn girl," Nancy replied.

"I can hear it slightly in your accent."

"Oh! Good. I thought maybe I'd lost too much of my accent. It's like losing your identity, isn't it?"

Linda agreed somberly. She shifted her weight, suddenly nervous, then said, "Well. I have a meeting with Dr. Grimson in a little while."

"My daughter is a genius," Nancy shot with a wide smile. "Just be honest with her about your health journey. She'll guide you."

An hour and a half later, Linda found herself within Janine Grimson's office, with its dark-purple curtains, Moroccan rug, and a beautiful antique map of the world. A candle brewed a scent Linda didn't recognize, something that seemed to slow her anxious thoughts, much like the yoga had. Janine pulsed through the door and delivered a beautiful smile, one that captivated Linda and reminded her all over again of Nancy's kindness. It was a funny thing, having seen Janine Potter through the pages of tabloid magazines, only to have her fully-formed, three-dimensional before her. She was far prettier in person, although Linda knew better than to say that. It would only come off strangely.

"Good morning! It looks like you've just arrived the night before last?"

"That's right."

"From... the city?"

"That's right," Linda repeated, feeling dull at her lack of creativity.

"Wonderful. Me too." Janine adjusted herself on the seat across from Linda and scribed something on a little yellow pad of paper. "Now, I'm sure you've read all about our clinic here at the Lodge, but I just want to start by telling you a bit about naturopathy and our commitment to wellness. In many ways, the diseases and discomforts within our body can be healed without the use of drugs. We consider your diet, your exercise, your mental health, among other things, and create a clean path forward."

Linda nodded as her throat tightened. "I guess it's true that a pill always seemed too easy to me."

Janine chuckled kindly. "Unfortunately, wellness isn't all that easy. It's a lifelong journey and one we should be excited about, as it always brings us closer to ourselves."

Closer? To herself? Linda had very little desire for whatever that meant. Still, here she sat before Janine Potter. She would fake it as much as she could.

"Now, to get started on our journey together, I'd like to get a better feel for your life back in the city," Janine began. "Why don't you tell me a bit about your background, your family, your schedule... that kind of thing."

Linda's brain felt inflamed. *How could she possibly tell this beautiful woman that she hadn't had a friend in over a decade? How could she say that she'd eaten Cream of Wheat every morning for as long as she could remember?*

"I don't know quite where to be," Linda replied, fiddling with her hands in her lap.

Janine's cheek twitched slightly. "What about your family? Easy to start there."

Linda shook her head so that her hair wafted across the upper parts of her shoulders. "I don't have any family to speak of."

Janine's eyes grew shadowed. Quickly, Linda added, "I had the opportunity to have a family a long time ago. But things grew complicated. It's a long story. It's just hard to explain."

"I can understand complication if you give me a shot," Janine breathed.

"No. It's not necessary." Linda scrambled to fill the space between them. "Other than that, I've spent the past few months working at a high-end retailer in Manhattan. I recently left that position and am curious about the next steps to take in my life. My diet is quite bland and standard, although I haven't struggled with my weight at all in several decades and I normally get enough sleep."

None of these issues seemed to hit the real problems at hand. Still, Janine scribbled the notes to herself as Linda spoke. Perhaps this would be enough. After a long moment's pause, Janine lifted her head.

"We have several treatment options for you over the next twelve days," Janine explained. "Along with a very nutritionally balanced diet, which I think will ignite your energy levels and start the healing process. Beyond that, we can offer acupuncture, therapy sessions, yoga, spa treatments, and meditation sessions."

Linda forced herself to nod along with each addition.

"But beyond that, I have to say..." Janine placed her yellow pad of paper off to the side and laced her fingers together. "It's essential for us to feel a part of our society. It's essential that we feel companionship. Your body craves it. The fact that you're here at the Lodge means that you've been neglecting yourself in some way. I hope that when you return to the city, you'll take a hard look at your daily routine and try to give yourself kindness and compassion. I hope you'll reach out to people you've known before or work to make new friends. Community centers can be good for that, as can social media groups with weekly meet-ups."

Linda's throat tightened. She wanted to tell Janine just how little strength she had for something like that.

"You said you had the option to have a family," Janine continued. "Do you feel a lot of regret around that?"

Didn't Janine sense that Linda didn't want to discuss this? That it was a sore spot within her soul?

"Not really," Linda lied. "I think it's just how things had to go."

Janine's eyes shimmered. She then turned back toward her computer, where she typed in Linda's details. Linda studied the floor as her cheeks warmed with embarrassment.

"I'll have a schedule ready for you within the hour," Janine informed her a moment later. "Mallory will drop it off in your room. I look forward to working with you over the next twelve days. And I hope..."

Linda arched an eyebrow as Janine stuttered through what she wanted to say.

"I hope we'll find ways to talk about what's going on in your life," Janine finally added. "Because I do believe honesty, while difficult, is the only way forward."

Linda wandered back to her room after that. She felt as though she'd been punched in the stomach. Janine Potter, before seen only from the glossy pages of a magazine, had tried her darnedest to see all the way through Linda. She'd seen the glimmer of darkness.

Once perched on her bed, Linda grabbed her old notebook from her backpack and flipped through the pages. The only photo she still had from that time period crept out from between the pages and fluttered to the bedspread.

There they were: a family of three. A twenty-something Linda as she held a four-month-old baby and grinned madly at the camera, her smile the exact brightness of sunshine. The man beside her held her around the waist. In the photo, he seemed their protector.

Was this the last time Linda had felt true happiness? Or had she created it all in her mind, something to return to for comfort? It was difficult to say.

Chapter Eight

From the backseat of Kelli Montgomery's real estate van, Maggie stretched out her aching legs and listened to the cadence of conversation between Kelli, Janine, and Maxine. They drove along the southern coast of Martha's Vineyard as the December sunlight cascaded through the windows and danced across their cheeks. Maxine was wide-eyed with wonder over the story of Kelli and her recent sale of the Aquinnah Cliffside Overlook Hotel, an old-world hotel on the western edge of the island, which had been destroyed by a hurricane in 1943.

"But the weird thing is, my grandfather sold the place to the man my grandmother was married to," Kelli explained as she drove them toward the fourth of six houses she planned to show off to Maxine that afternoon.

"Oh my! So when did your grandmother leave this other man?" Maxine asked excitedly.

"Around the same time," Kelli affirmed. "But all this just came out a little while ago. Family secrets galore."

"You divide your time between the real estate business and your boutique, don't you?" Janine asked Kelli. "I just love that place."

"To be honest with you, my daughter has taken over most of the boutique responsibilities," Kelli continued. "My new boyfriend is the man behind the reconstruction of the Aquinnah Cliffside, and I find myself out on the construction site more often than not. It's so exciting to see it all come together. It's beyond my wildest dreams to dig into the past and build this new reality from the old world."

Kelli parked the real estate van outside a moderate-sized mansion just a mile or so west of where Elsa had raised her children with her now-deceased husband, Aiden. Janine, Maxine, and Maggie stepped into the chilly light and followed Kelli up to the front door.

"This house just went on the market," Kelli explained. "It's three bedrooms, two bathrooms, with a picture-perfect view of the beach and access to the neighboring woods."

"And not too far from us," Janine added pointedly.

Maggie followed them through the marble-floored foyer into the living area with its bay window that glowed with a beautiful view of the Atlantic Ocean just beyond. The ocean had tamed since Maggie's arrival; the waves lapped in a friendly manner over the sands.

"Three bedrooms seems a bit much, doesn't it?" Maxine asked Janine as they headed for the kitchen.

"Who knows where life might lead you?" Janine pointed out. "You might want to receive guests here."

Maxine chuckled, but not unkindly. "Janny, you're the only person in my life these days."

Janine blushed and opened a kitchen cabinet. "Lots of space for kitchen supplies."

"Right. Because I'm always cooking, as you know," Maxine teased.

"It is a lot of space," Kelli offered, trying to be understanding of her client's needs. "I have a number of smaller properties, of course."

"Oh, this is simply wonderful to look at," Maxine said hurriedly. "I'm just trying to figure out the next stages of my life. Considering renting out my place in Manhattan and trying out island life more full-time. It's a huge leap, though."

"There's no rush with these kinds of things," Kelli assured her. "If you don't feel the pull toward a place, we can move on to the next one. Property purchases normally rise around springtime. I imagine this place will stay on the market until then."

Maxine and Janine stood in front of the large bay window and gazed out across the stands. They discussed various ways to construct the backyard and whether or not it would be appropriate to put in a pool. Maggie couldn't help but think that the house was perfectly stellar for a young family of three or four. How often had she told Rex they would have to find something different when they had their second child, as theirs was only a two-bedroom apartment? How many children had she planned for in this amorphous, non-future? Had she really pictured her and Rex as the parents of four, maybe five children? It seemed laughable now.

"What do you think, Mags?" This was Maxine, who flashed her a magazine-ready smile as she turned around. "Could you see me here?"

"Um. Yes?"

Maxine laughed good-naturedly. "It's too big. I know that." She turned to face Kelli and asked to move on to the next place. "I'm in no real rush. The place in downtown Edgartown is cozy enough for now. And you're right. I want it to be perfect."

They investigated two more less-than-perfect properties before Kelli dropped them back at the real estate office in Oak Bluffs. They piled again in Janine's car as Maxine expressed the desire for a "small glass of wine." They headed for an Edgartown Wine Bar and parked just outside as snow began to flutter around them.

Once inside, Janine ordered them a single bottle of Primitivo with three glasses. Maggie realized she hadn't said a single word in over ten minutes. Maxine's eyes found hers and glimmered with curiosity.

"How are you doing these days, Mags? How is that handsome husband of yours?"

"Just fine." What did people expect her to say?

"You must have a packed social calendar in the city for the holidays," Maxine continued. "I remember my mid-twenties well. It seemed that every day, I was on a quest to find the perfect outfit for the night's cocktail party. It was exhausting, and I lived for it."

"Remember that one party? We were maybe twenty-six, twenty-seven, and you spilled wine all over that woman's dress?" Janine asked brightly.

"Oh gosh. She wasn't just any woman. She was my date's mother..." Maxine blushed at the memory. "She told me I would never outgrow my Brooklyn roots and informed her son that if he continued to see me, she would disown him."

"Did he stop seeing you?" Janine exclaimed.

"I mean, formally, yes. He still popped up every once in a while..." Maxine added mischievously.

Maggie was more like her mother. She couldn't understand the exhilarating nature of dating around. Alyssa was more like Maxine and Grandma Nancy in this way. She saw dating as this beautiful patchwork of different experiences. Maggie was a romantic. Maggie's heart, even now, ached for only one man, Rex.

Each had a glass of wine before Janine grumbled that she had to make a pit stop at the Lodge to grab a few papers. "I have to go over some things tonight, unfortunately," she sighed.

"Well, thank you for going around with me to look at these properties," Maxine told her. "I appreciated the company from both of you."

"You mind if we stop by the Lodge?" Janine asked Maggie, who'd very nearly faded out of the conversation entirely.

"No, I don't mind at all," Maggie recited, just a moment too late.

Maxine walked back to her downtown Edgartown apartment, gliding through the snow as though she walked through a dream. Maggie slid into the passenger seat of her mother's car and snapped on her seatbelt.

"Is it really okay with you that Maxine stays on the island?" Maggie asked pointedly.

Janine turned up the radio. "You can deal with it however you want. I've found my own way."

This shut Maggie up all the way to the Lodge. She recognized her inner sorrows had begun to manifest as sharp-edged remarks to others. This wasn't her personality, more a marred version. Once at the Lodge, she stepped into the foyer to greet Mallory, who was about to depart for the day.

"Lucas wants to have another talk about getting back together," Mallory grumbled inwardly.

Maggie had to bite her tongue not to tell her, *don't do it.*

"What are you going to say?" Maggie asked.

"I'm going to tell him I'm still thinking about it. And also, that I've enjoyed this time apart. It's given me space to consider my new life as a mother and what kind of mother I want to be. I certainly don't want to be the mother I was when we lived together. All we did was fight. I was exhausted constantly. I had nothing to give Zachery. Now, especially with all of you around, I feel an understanding of love and companionship I'd forgotten when I was with Lucas."

"Maybe that's all you need right now," Maggie breathed.

"Maybe."

With Mallory gone, Maggie wandered through the halls of the Lodge, which flowed with beautiful and bright-faced women, each on a different day of their mental, emotional, and physical health journeys— and each armed with enough green smoothies to feed a small army. They spoke with what seemed to be enlightenment about their new discoveries about their personalities and tendencies and how they planned to "work on themselves" after leaving the Lodge. Maggie wanted to pick fun at them but found, instead, that she was jealous of them. Her insides were sour. She worried she would never find the light again.

Maggie strolled into the kitchen, where the chef greeted her warmly and gestured for the oven. "I've made cookies. If you wait around another four minutes, you can have one fresh from the oven."

Maggie grinned sheepishly. "I imagine they're nutritional and sugar-free?"

The chef nodded. "But you know I put my magic touch in them. You won't notice a thing."

The chef was correct. With the first bite, Maggie's eyes closed as pleasure rolled across her taste buds. "You've done it again," she breathed as the chef giggled with excitement. "Grab a few more before I sound the alarm. The minute these women catch wind of fresh cookies, they'll be gone."

Maggie grabbed two more, thanked the chef, and headed back out into the enormous dining hall, with its glowing windows. Dusk had fallen into darkness, and the sharp sliver of the moon glittered its light across the waves of Katama Bay. Only a few women remained in the dining area, chatting over juices or tea, some with clay masks plastered across their faces. All wore soft pink robes, the kind the Lodge gave you when you checked in.

Toward the far corner, a woman sat alone and gazed out the window at the waves beyond. She wore a pink robe and a pair of slippers and hovered a pen over a notebook. Her grey-blonde hair was styled simply, and she'd removed her makeup, which revealed a fresh and sweet face, one that looked to be in its mid-sixties. This made her a bit older than most of the other guests at the Lodge. Maggie wondered if this was why the woman kept her distance from the others. Was she embarrassed about her age? Did she just lack understanding of what to say?

Maggie stepped over to the woman. As she made her way closer, the woman sensed her and scrunched her face with confusion. She even turned her head around to look behind her, as though certain that Maggie was en route to someone else.

Maggie slipped a cookie onto a spare napkin and placed it before the woman. "I just wanted to make sure you got one before the others pounced on them," she said simply.

The woman blinked up at her with confusion. Probably, she'd

sat by herself on purpose— armor from a social reality she didn't want. But after a pause, she lifted the cookie and took a small bite.

"Oh. Goodness." The woman lifted her eyebrows. "The next thing you'll tell me is it doesn't have any sugar in it."

"It doesn't," Maggie affirmed with a smile.

"Ridiculous," the woman countered. "I need this recipe. It's divine."

"The chef has told me several times that she'll never reveal her secrets."

The woman lent her a soft smile as she positioned the rest of the cookie on the napkin, as though she wanted to savor it. The chef called to the other women in face masks that she had a fresh batch of cookies. Like hyenas, they scuttled to the source of food and grabbed them as Maggie and the woman before her shared a giggle.

"I take it you don't know any of them?" Maggie asked.

"I keep to myself, I suppose," the woman said. "My naturopath doctor says I have a whole lot of work to do. I'm trying to write some stuff down to make sense of my life."

Maggie sensed such sorrow behind her words. She decided not to tell the woman that her mother was Janine Grimson Potter, her doctor. She didn't want to complicate things.

"I've never made sense of anything," Maggie replied simply.

"Yes, well. I suppose I didn't have much of anything figured out at your age," the woman told her with the smallest of smiles. After a strange pause, she leafed through her journal and drew out an old photograph, which featured a beautiful twenty-something woman who carried a small baby. Beside her, a truly handsome, twenty-something man had his arms around her, an act of protection. Their smiles were electric, without fear.

"I was around your age here, I think," the woman told her.

"You're so beautiful," Maggie breathed.

The woman's eyes watered. "It was a perfect moment in an otherwise imperfect life. Perhaps I should have given more thought to things back then. Perhaps I should have looked at the big picture. I don't know." A single tear fell, which she hurriedly wiped away.

Maggie's heart shattered at the sight. Whatever had happened in this woman's past, she had a hunch it wasn't terribly happy. Had the husband left? Had the baby died? Maggie dropped her chin to her chest and exhaled all the air from her lungs.

And without fully comprehending why she did it, she found herself telling this stranger the truth.

"I just found out that I can't have children. It's all I've wanted since I can remember. And I don't even know how to talk about it. I can't even tell my husband."

The woman's shoulders fell forward with sorrow. She placed the photo back in her journal and reached for Maggie's wrist, which she held tenderly. They held the silence of their joint pain for a long moment.

Finally, the woman spoke.

"All my life, I've run from pain. But it's caught up to me, over and over again. It's been the monster hiding under my bed."

Maggie wondered if this woman could see how much Maggie wanted to run from her pain, too. Was it that apparent?

"Whatever this means to you, I hope you find the strength to stare it in the face," the woman continued softly. "I hope you find a way to carry it with you without letting it destroy you. I hope you will not end up like me: a very lonely woman in the corner writing in her journal about her past regrets."

79

"Maggie? You ready?"

Maggie glanced back to find her mother coming toward her with a file folder under her arm. She grinned broadly as her eyes found the stranger in the corner.

"Linda! I see you've met my daughter."

Linda's eyes widened as she shifted outward to face Janine. "She's quite a remarkable woman. She just snuck me a cookie from the kitchen before the others got to them."

Janine's eyes shimmered with confusion, but her smile did not falter. "Oh gosh. Are those the chocolate avocado ones? I hope I'm not too late..."

"They've been pounced on, I'm afraid," Maggie replied as she turned her eyes toward Linda's. She hoped her expression translated just how much she wasn't ready to tell her mother her truth. Somehow, Linda seemed to accept this in stride.

"Too bad. Well. I hope you have a nice rest tonight, Linda! It was so wonderful to meet you this morning," Janine stated as she stepped back.

"Good night, Linda," Maggie said softly as she joined her mother.

Once outside the Lodge, Janine positioned her file folder in the back seat and adjusted herself in the driver's side. "That woman is so lonely, I think," she commented with a heavy sigh. "I asked her about her life in the city, and she seemed to suggest that any kind of social life was a thing of her deep past. I can help her here and now, but two weeks from now? A month? I just imagine her on the streets of Manhattan, cold and alone. It breaks my heart."

Maggie marveled at the weight of loneliness within Linda, a

woman who carried around an old photograph from a bygone era as her final link to some sort of happiness.

"What kind of decisions lead you to that, do you think?" she asked her mother now.

"Oh, gosh. Life just weaves and winds, doesn't it? It's hard to say what led her here. It fills me with such gratefulness to know we have that big house of love back home."

Chapter Nine

"I won't do it. I won't have an engagement party. Cody and I have known each other for decades. What is there to celebrate?"

"Carm! Listen to yourself. You and Cody have every reason to celebrate. You finally found one another after so many years of will-they, won't they. He asked you to marry him for crying out loud. Why won't you let us celebrate?" Elsa stomped around the kitchen and began to scribe a long list of items for this supposed "party."

Maggie and Alyssa smeared butter across English muffins at the kitchen nook breakfast table and eyed one another with good humor. It was better than daytime television. All they had to do was run downstairs and "turn on" the unscripted series of "What Will Carmella and Elsa Disagree About Today?"

"I just can't stand it. All these people standing around and watching us and asking us..."

"What? Tell me, Carm. What's the inevitable conclusion of a

beautiful holiday engagement party? You worried the food will be too good? You worried everyone will have a brilliant time?" Elsa demanded.

Carmella dropped her teeth into her lower lip and hummed inwardly.

"I think the battle might already be lost, Aunt Carm." Alyssa sipped her mug of black coffee and lifted her English muffin as a sort of salute.

"Don't you think it'll be marvelous?" Elsa demanded of Maggie and Alyssa as she placed her hands on her hips.

"Marvelous is the word for it," Alyssa confirmed. "For the rest of us, at least. Carmella, if you find a place to hide in the hall closet, I'll sneak you snacks and wine."

"I knew I could count on you, honey." For the first time that morning, Carmella's face broke open into a smile like a cracked egg. It glowed, genuine and sweet. Perhaps she wanted the party after all and simply had to resist Elsa's advancements due to old habits.

"I think we should just have it tomorrow. Get it over with before the full-blown holiday festivities take over," Elsa suggested, distracted as she continued to write up a list of grocery items and decorations. "Are you and Cody free?"

"I guess we'll have to be." Carmella flipped her dark locks and shared a secret smile with Alyssa, who giggled into her mug of coffee.

All this talk of engagement parties made Maggie's stomach twist. Flashbacks from her own engagement party raced through her mind. It had been an elaborate event on a rooftop in Manhattan and ultimately culminated in the "surprise!" shock that her mother's best friend had frequent relations with her father. Talk about whiplash! Talk about a party to remember! Could Carmella's compete with that?

As though he'd sensed her reckless thoughts, Rex chose this moment to call. Maggie leaped up to answer it in the living room. As she scampered away, Alyssa called, "Get back here quick before I eat your English muffin, too!"

"What was Alyssa yelling about?" Rex started with laughter.

Maggie's heart quickened at the mere sound of his voice. Things had been strained between them since her departure to the island. While normally they might have spoken once a day, they'd neglected one another and called once every two, if that. She ached with missing him yet also viewed him as synonymous with the greatest sorrow of her life, one she couldn't yet face.

"You know Alyssa. She's always yelling about something." She swallowed to loosen her tight throat and then added, "How is, um. How is everything?" What did she mean by everything, anyway? His "important" business meetings? His career? Their friends? What? It all felt at such distance from her.

"Oh, it's good. I just received news that the promotion should come through by the beginning of the year."

"That's fantastic news." Her voice remained flat.

"I'd love to come to visit you. Tomorrow or... Or whatever you want."

There was a sharp urgency to his words. Was he frightened she wouldn't return?

"It's just that I've been thinking," he continued. "I know how important it is to you, and to me, to start a family. Now that the promotion is a for-sure thing, I'm totally on board."

"I see."

In the kitchen, Carmella howled something about the engagement party's list being entirely too long. "I'm an introvert, Elsa. I hardly even want you there!"

"Are you having second thoughts about having kids?" Rex asked pointedly.

Maggie couldn't speak. In all their years of dating and engagement and, now, marriage, Maggie had never kept a secret from Rex. They had swapped tales of love and loss over their pillows deep into the night. It had felt miraculous to find a partner who appreciated whispered gossip.

"I have to go, Rex," Maggie said.

"Maggie... When are you coming back? I want to set up the tree. I want to have a little Christmas with you. Here in our apartment."

The edges of Maggie's heart shattered. This was their first Christmas as husband and wife. She twisted her wedding band around and around her fourth finger. It seemed suddenly so heavy.

"I promise you. I'll be back soon," she told him softly.

"Good. Good." He replied quickly, as though afraid she was about to take her promise back. "I love you, Maggie."

"I love you, too."

When Maggie turned back toward the kitchen, she found herself face-to-face with a stern-looking Alyssa. She lowered her eyebrows and crossed her arms over her chest.

"Maggie. What the hell is going on?"

Maggie slid a strand of hair behind her ear. "What do you mean?"

"I mean, all the blood just drained from your face. You've looked on the verge of tears ever since that evening out in Brooklyn. I feel like you're not being honest with me. I feel..."

"It's all fine," Maggie told her. "Seriously. I'm just, you know. Recharging after Dad and everything." How simple it now was to lie to everyone she held dear. It was just like anything else— you had to practice at it. Practice made perfect.

The following evening, true to her word, Elsa held an intimate engagement party for Carmella and Cody. The holiday decor served the house well for the affair, with dangling mistletoes hung in several corners, glowing ribbons, and a large banner, which read, "CONGRATULATIONS, CODY AND CARM." During the hours leading up to the event itself, Elsa barked orders at whoever marched into her wake, with her boyfriend, Bruce, picking up the majority of the slack.

Dinner was served at seven-thirty. Carmella and Cody sat at the head of the table, with toddler Gretchen seated alongside them, her curls wilder than ever and her laughter frenetic. The rest of their family and friends crammed around the table, giggling with tipsiness and excitement. Elsa rose to deliver a speech, her glass of champagne lifted.

"We've been through much, you and I, Carmella," she began. "Nobody would say it's been an easy road. But I've felt genuine love from you every step of the way. No matter what happened, I knew we had one another's backs. The past few years, since we lost both Aiden and Dad, we've floundered a great deal. But now, we find ourselves here, in the very house where we grew up. We fight and we laugh and we cry, and we do it all together. To watch you take this beautiful next step with your best friend and true love, Cody... it breaks my heart and gives me hope, all at once. I know we're entering a brand-new era. And I know that we'll have one another's backs, through thick and thin."

After dinner, Bruce started a bonfire out on the shoreline. The fire flickered and spat, casting an orange glow that fought against the dark December evening. It was strangely warm for the season, upper-forties, and everyone crowded around with piping-hot wine in mugs and enough excitement to brew up several hours of conversation. Maggie felt at a distance from everyone, her tongue heavy. She stared beyond the flames to the spewing waves beyond. She resented the way she'd treated Rex recently and burned with self-hatred. This was a family party, and Rex should have been there. As it stood, she hadn't invited him.

"Hey, girl." Alyssa stepped up and shoved Maggie with a pointed elbow. "You good?"

"Never better." Maggie sipped her wine and pointed her nose toward her mother and Henry, who cuddled against one another on a nearby log. "Mom's in love, huh?"

Alyssa cackled. "She's like a teenage girl with a crush. I'll never forget how she forced us to drive across Spain and Portugal just so she could go tell him she loved him."

"It was like a rom-com," Maggie agreed. Her heart lifted. This was the way she was accustomed to speaking with Alyssa. Perhaps this was what acting normal felt like. Perhaps she could find her way through.

"Would you drive across Europe to track down Rex?" Alyssa asked.

"In a heartbeat," Maggie told her. In a moment, guilt folded over her. She finished her mug of wine and turned herself back toward the house. "I think I'll grab some more wine. You want some?"

Alyssa passed her mug over and nodded before heading over to Cole, Elsa's eldest son, whom Alyssa had grown closer to over the previous month. Maggie shot out from the warmth of the brewing fire and jumped back onto the closed porch before heading into the kitchen.

Once there, however, she heard the volatile hum of familiar voices in the midst of what seemed to be a horrible argument. Poised at the countertop, she craned to hear. Before long, she recognized that the voices were, in fact, Mallory and Lucas's. Lucas had been a member at the table for dinner. He and Mallory had sat on either side of Zachery, who had positioned himself upright in his little highchair and smashed his plastic spoon against his counter. Throughout, Maggie had avoided Lucas's gaze. Their recent fight hadn't filled her with warm-and-fuzzy feelings.

Maggie stepped closer to the hallway. It was perhaps shameful, prying into their private relationship like this. To put it simply, she didn't trust Lucas— not in the slightest and wanted to ensure Mallory was all right.

"I just don't understand. You've been here long enough, haven't you? Six months? Seven?" Lucas demanded.

Mallory's voice seemed so humble and sweet when compared to his. "I just think it's healthy for Zach and me to be here with my mom for now."

"You said that before. You said you needed time to think."

"And I still need that time..." Mallory stuttered.

"It's ridiculous, Mallory. You've destroyed our family. We're always trading Zach back and forth like a football. I hate it. It's not the way things were supposed to go."

Maggie's throat tightened with fear.

"You were supposed to move back in. You were supposed to

be there to support me. You were..." Lucas continued to lay into her.

"I just can't right now," Mallory whispered. "It's too soon."

"Just say what you mean, Mallory. Say you want Zachery to be unhappy. Say that..."

Maggie couldn't help herself. Guided by an unknown, immovable force, she stormed into the living room and interrupted Lucas's horrible rant. Mallory's cheeks were blotchy and tear-streaked.

"Hey, Lucas. I think it might be time for you to leave," Maggie fumed, her hands on her hips as she stared straight at him.

Lucas's eyes widened in surprise. He looked on the verge of saying something monstrous, but he instead turned his eyes toward Mallory as he said, "This isn't over." He then stormed out toward the foyer, where he collected his coat. All the while, Maggie and Mallory stood with bated breath. He slammed the door behind him and left them in sinister silence. That moment, Mallory let out a strange sob. Maggie took one stride and wrapped her arms around Mallory. In the corner, little Zachery slept on, oblivious to his parents' anger.

Maggie pulled back, gripping Mallory's shoulders. "You're worth so much more than the way he treats you," she told her softly. "You know that, right?"

Mallory swiped a hand over her cheek. It was one thing to say these words; it was a far different thing to believe them. Maggie knew this well, especially after so many years of her father scolding her. It was easy to think you deserved that.

"If you don't want to go back to him, you shouldn't even consider it. Not even if he threatens you," Maggie continued.

Mallory's lower lip quivered. "He's right about one thing. I always wanted us to be a family. I wanted Zachery to have both of his parents."

"He does have both of his parents. It just doesn't look the way you initially planned. That isn't your fault."

Alyssa appeared in the hall between the kitchen and the living room. Her eyes searched through the grey light to find Maggie with her hands latched over Mallory's shoulders. Her lips parted in surprise.

"Okay. Okay," she stuttered. "What did that jerk do this time?"

Nearly an hour later, with Zachery up in his crib alone, Mallory sat in the quietness of the back porch with the baby monitor on her lap and a large mug of mulled wine before her. Maggie and Alyssa sat on either side and continued to console her about her decision never to return to Lucas, no matter how lonely that decision felt. Out beyond the porch, the engagement party continued into the night. Cody flung his arm around Carmella's shoulders and held her tightly against him as the firelight caught the curve of her smile.

"It's been weird watching Aunt Carmella the past few months," Mallory breathed. "She was always so introverted and sometimes awkward. Now, it's like she's found herself. And I have this huge fear that I won't find my true self until my forties, either."

Maggie's heart dropped into the pit of her stomach. "Maybe it's not about when it happens. It's more about the journey. At least, that's what I hope for."

Alyssa grumbled inwardly. "In my mind, both of you have a whole lot figured out. You've got your son. And Maggie, you've got Rex and plan to have a baby of your own soon. Me? I'm like a ship out to sea without a captain."

Mallory giggled as Maggie's stomach twisted with sorrow.

"Just because I had a baby doesn't mean I know anything more about being in my twenties than you do," Mallory pointed out.

"And just because I got married doesn't mean I'm any less lost," Maggie countered.

Alyssa shrugged. "Where do you think I should take this weird life of mine? Should I stay on the Vineyard? Head back to the city?" She slid her palms together as her eyes widened. "I feel like there are so many possibilities before me, and I don't feel especially drawn to any of them. I guess that's why I wanted things to work with that Dutchman so badly. I thought to myself; finally, I can just fall in love..."

"And everything always works out when you fall in love," Mallory returned sarcastically.

Alyssa laughed sadly. "Gosh, I'm sorry about that guy. He's still young. Men grow up much later than us women. Maybe he'll be an okay father for Zachery, at least— even if he isn't the one for you."

Mallory nodded as her eyes flickered with sorrow. "I don't know if I can love him anymore. But you're right. His relationship with Zachery is all that matters now. As long as we're there for him in every way... As long as we give him mountains of love... Our failed relationship doesn't matter. Not in the slightest."

Chapter Ten

The weekend's warmth took a sharp downward turn and cast the island in another white blanket of snow. Linda awoke on Monday morning just in time for yoga and blinked out at the shimmering white as it continued its glorious flurry from cloud to earth. Once outside of Nancy's yoga studio, she listened to the whimsical conversations between the other Lodge ladies. They all spoke about this "most magical" time of year with a certainty that made Linda almost believe. Three of the ladies even greeted Linda by name, probably remembering her as the "older woman who kept to herself." This didn't bother Linda. In reality, it was just remarkable to be remembered. It was remarkable to be known.

After yoga, Linda returned to her room for a quick shower. Once back on her bedspread, wrapped up in a fluffy towel, she recorded her thoughts in her journal— grateful that her outlook had shifted since her arrival.

December 13, 2021

It feels to me that there is every reason to be hopeful, despite all the trauma of previous lives.

Perhaps I can be someone new.

Perhaps I don't have to be alone.

That isn't too much to dream for, is it?

Breakfast began at eight. Linda donned a pair of jeans and a zip-up sweatshirt and walked down the antique, circular staircase, which led to the large open-air dining hall, which bustled with life and vibrant conversation from the lively awoken Lodge residents. The vegan breakfast of green smoothies, homemade bread, vegan jams, plenty of vegetables, and little vegan snacks, awaited to fuel them for their therapeutic schedule ahead. Linda's afternoon was frightening and exhilarating, as she had finally agreed to take on Carmella Remington's acupuncture— something she'd heard would relax her mind and body in ways she couldn't fully comprehend.

A green smoothie in hand, Linda stepped toward a single table near the window, which allowed her the comfort of being in a crowded room without the necessity of making conversation. Every day brought a different sort of fear, a different sort of challenge. Linda thought that, perhaps, she would one day find the strength to broach her version of small talk. Maybe she would even, one day, find a way to make new friends.

However, when the crowd in front of her parted, Linda found herself privy to a very surprising sight.

There before her, between the dining hall and the hallway in the distance, stood Janine Grimson Potter alongside her best friend, the Brooklynite Maxine Aubert. It was as though they'd stepped out of the pages of the glossy magazine that Linda had read. They both wore top-notch fashion, better designs, even than DENISE ever would have hung up on their racks. Maxine's blonde-tinged hair flowed beautifully across her shoulders, and her winter coat was fluffed with snow, as though she'd only just entered. Her lipstick shone bright red, like an apple plucked from a tree, and her eyes danced with humor as Janine spoke.

Janine flashed her head around to catch Linda, whose own eyes were wide as saucers. Janine's smile didn't skip a beat. She waved toward Linda in a friendly manner, which led Linda to wave her green smoothie back. Janine and Maxine stepped toward her, their expensive boots clacking beneath them. Linda felt foolish in her jeans and zip-up. She tried out a smile that immediately faltered.

"Good morning," Janine greeted. "How's the smoothie today?"

Linda wrapped her lips around the straw foolishly and sucked just enough to taste. "Oh, it's really good," she replied.

"We should grab one." Janine turned to Maxine.

"Oh yes. I would love it," Maxine returned. Her voice lilted just the slightest bit with what was left of a French accent. Her eyes hardly graced Linda's before she stepped around Janine and joined the green smoothie line.

"Enjoy your morning, Linda. Acupuncture later?" Janine asked as she headed forward to join Maxine.

This left Linda among strangers, who swarmed around her like buzzing bees in a nest. Her throat tightened strangely. The green smoothie in her hand now seemed silly. *How could she possibly heal her entire heart and mind with a single pulsed-up spinach drink? How could she possibly undo decades of heartache with a two-week retreat? Why on earth was she there?*

Behind her, Maxine cackled at something Janine said. Their friendship glowed as bright as the sun that had long ago disappeared behind the winter clouds. Linda was reminded yet again of her loneliness. She hurried past the trash can, deposited her green drink, then sped back to her bedroom. Her mind raced sporadically. She was reminded of that last evening at DENISE when her mind had taken over completely and she'd fallen into a panic that had changed her life forever.

No job. No prospects. Using up what was left of her savings.

Why?

She spent the morning back in bed as the snow piled on outside. When the time came for her acupuncture appointment, she latched her door and shut off her phone, avoiding Carmella altogether. At four, she snuck back into the hallway, donned her winter coat, and flagged down one of the Lodge van drivers with a request.

"Would you mind taking me to town?" she asked as sweetly as she could, although she could hardly even hear her voice. She felt as though she hovered somewhere above herself, as though she existed in a vacuum in another world, watching as her body took itself from place to place.

How silly she felt. *Why had she come there? Why had she imagined that everything would be all right?*

Once in downtown Edgartown, the driver explained that the Edgartown Christmas Market was up and running, with plenty of kiosks that contained "sinful" mulled wine and various Christmas snacks that made your mouth water.

"It's not vegan stuff," the driver told her with a laugh. "But it's good enough to make the cheat worth it."

Linda laughed. "Don't tell on me."

"I would never." The driver gave her his card to make sure she would call him back to be taken to the Lodge after she was done with her "Christmas shopping," which was the excuse she'd come up with for the trip.

Once outside, Linda shoved her hands into her coat pockets as snow piled up across the curve of her greying locks and the city of Edgartown flowed around her, yet another reminder that no matter where she went, she was still just as alone as ever before.

Linda paused at a mulled wine stand, where she purchased a mug of steaming-hot liquid from a bright-eyed blonde woman of maybe twenty-five. Linda asked the woman for the time, and she said it was nearly four-thirty, which was a "good enough time to start drinking." Linda tried to laugh at her joke but found it difficult to form her lips around it. Instead, she paid, walked out of the crowd toward a nearby bench, and drank the entire thing in four big gulps. Her head swam, but the sharpness of her thoughts seemed to ease.

Now, the bigger questions didn't bother her so much, like, whether or not she would ever make it back to New York City, or whether or not she'd made every possible mistake throughout her life, or whether or not the love she'd had in her life had ever been real. None of it mattered. Now, as her breath turned to white fog before her and the snow swirled around where she sat, she knew that no matter what she did, time would continue on its merry way.

She purchased another mug of mulled wine from a different vendor to test out the different tastes. This time, she walked around with her wine and watched the other passers-by, the couples young and old who seemed willing to walk arm-in-arm and giggle together, their cheeks bright with chill. Linda had only been in love once. Sometimes, she searched for that love within her, as though she had misplaced it the way you might misplace a magazine or a cell phone. *Was it under her heart? Was it between other memories in her mind? Or was love something that went away if you didn't continue to cultivate it?*

These were questions she couldn't answer. Not with just two mugs of mulled wine, anyway. As the evening light dimmed around her, she shot for her third mulled wine stand and ordered as her smile widened from ear to ear. In the distance, the Edgartown Marching Band played a collection of Christmas hits, mostly out-of-tune, although nobody seemed to care. That was the thing about kids. They could do basically anything half-well and you still appreciated it. Linda even remembered that from her brief time with a child of her own. Any drawing the child had made, Linda had called it "better than Monet could have ever done" and hung it on the fridge with excitement. She'd known her child would excel and had no thoughts otherwise.

It had been a very long time since Linda's child had been a child.

It had been a very long time since Linda had felt that love in real-time.

Now, as Linda sucked down her third mug of mulled wine, the world around her began to dim. Her thoughts fumbled together and seemed to trip on one another. As though, to match them, her feet got all tied up beneath her. As a laugh curled out from her throat, she fell forward and lost her grip on her mug. A flash of deep red liquid, like blood, went over the snow as the crowd around her screeched with worry.

Linda hardly felt the impact of the cement beneath her. Before she knew it, she was all crumpled up as the snow fluttered over her. Her head pounded... but had she hit it, or was this just the result of all that drinking on an empty stomach? Her mind couldn't wage the seriousness of the situation. Her hands hunted for the cement beneath her, something that would help her spring back up. But her arms lacked strength, and her dizziness continued. Laughter fell out of her as she managed nothing else. Maybe she would die right there on the streets of Edgartown. Maybe that's why she'd seen Maxine and Janine in the pages of that magazine and drummed up this idea of another world.

Maybe it would all end here.

"Linda? Linda?" Someone hollered her name from above her, but Linda couldn't make out the voice, nor could she open her eyes to whoever it was. For all she knew, she imagined it. *After all, who did she truly know on Martha's Vineyard? Who did she truly know across the world? No one.*

Chapter Eleven

"How do you know her name?" Mallory blinked down at Maggie as Maggie tried to turn Linda tenderly onto her back. The older woman's cheeks were flushed and strange, and her eyelids shifted over her eyes as she fell into some sort of unconscious sleep. The snow flickered across her forehead, bangs, and eyelashes as Maggie hollered her name again. "Linda!" It felt strange to speak to this limp woman stretched out before her, as though she'd left her body altogether.

"Call an ambulance," Maggie instructed Alyssa, who gawked down at her. Hurriedly, she grabbed her phone and dialed, describing their location at the Edgartown Christmas Market, the eastern edge.

"What else should I say?" Alyssa demanded of Maggie. "What happened to her?"

In truth, Maggie hadn't a clue. "Just tell them to hurry."

Alyssa hung up the phone and crouched down beside the

older woman as her ruby red lips parted in sorrow. Maggie touched Linda's hands to find that they were ice-cold. She removed her gloves from her pocket and tried to slip the older woman's fingers into them but found it too difficult. She instead unraveled her scarf from her neck and wrapped it around and around Linda's hands.

The events of the previous sixty seconds now seemed a blur of horror. Maggie, Mallory, and Alyssa had stood in line for their second mug of mulled wine, falling yet again into the conversation they'd seemed to keep up ever since Mallory's official breakup from Lucas, which had occurred at Carmella's engagement party. Their question: how could they handle their twenty-something decade with confidence in a way that promoted future growth? How could they remain true to themselves as they dealt with questions of motherhood and relationships and careers?

Then, something had caught Maggie's eye, and she'd yanked herself around to find a semi-familiar face, as it had taken a horrible trajectory toward the cement below.

Linda.

The lonely woman from the Lodge.

The one who hadn't had a friend in sight.

"Come on, Linda," Maggie breathed as she rubbed at her scarf around the woman's hands. "Come back to us."

"I hear the ambulance," Alyssa said finally.

Maggie blinked up to see that a small crowd formed around them to gawk at poor Linda, who'd assuredly never been really "seen" by many as she'd marched through life alone. Maggie's heart grew enflamed with anger. This woman, unconscious before them all, was the only woman she'd felt comfortable enough to tell her infertility secret to. *What did it mean to find her like this at the Christmas Market? Was it fate?*

Maybe nothing really meant anything. Or maybe everything meant everything.

The EMT workers stormed through the crowd with their gurney lifted. Maggie leaped back to allow them to administer care to Linda. They had her on the gurney in a flash and then headed back toward the ambulance, which was along the eastern edge of the Christmas Market. The bright red lights seemed to mock the other Christmas lights across the market, as they were sterile against the coziness.

"Gosh. That was dramatic..." Alyssa stated.

Maggie staggered forward. Around them, the crowd dissipated as though everyone had already forgotten the poor woman.

"Maggie? What are you doing?" Alyssa demanded.

Mallory's eyes turned to orbs. "You want to follow after her?"

"I can't just leave her up there alone," Maggie informed them simply.

"You still haven't told us how you know her," Alyssa pointed out.

"I met her at the Lodge," Maggie explained softly. "She seemed so sad and so lost. I don't know..."

"Shouldn't we call Mom, then?" Alyssa demanded. "I mean, that woman is not our responsibility, Mags."

But Maggie couldn't hear her sister, not as she raced through the crowd, past the gash of red liquid where Linda had spilled her wine, and back toward Janine's car, which they had borrowed for the afternoon. Mallory hustled after her as Alyssa let out an exasperated, "Ugh. Fine."

Back at the car, Maggie cranked the heat as Mallory rubbed

her palms together. In the backseat, Alyssa buckled her seatbelt and again said, "But why you, Maggie? What makes you so important in this poor woman's world?"

Maggie eased them through the parking lot and out onto the bustling roads of Edgartown. There was something awful about Christmas traffic, as though everyone was in a rush to get the cheerful activities over with already. A car behind Maggie blared its horn so much that Maggie nearly leaped from her skin.

"This woman. Linda." Maggie exhaled all the air from her lungs as she pressed the gas again. "She showed me this photograph of herself and a baby and a man from decades ago. She seemed so sad, as though she'd missed out on something or made some kind of mistake. I mean, this is all we've talked about the past few days, right? We don't want to make any mistakes. We want to learn and grow and build our lives the way we've always dreamed of. Maybe Linda can help us..."

"You mean, you want to prod this woman for details on her mistakes from the safety of her hospital bed?" Alyssa demanded.

"No! No." Maggie shook her head wildly. "In actuality, I just want to be there for her. I think she really needs a friend."

This shut Alyssa up for the time being. After all, loneliness was something they'd all reckoned with in their own, unique way. Alyssa had certainly felt it during the hours in Madrid as she'd fully grasped the weight of what had happened to her in the sky above the Atlantic.

Maggie parked outside the hospital and burst out of the driver's side. Alyssa and Mallory scrambled after her as she charged toward the automatic doors of the Emergency Room. Maggie visualized that photograph Linda had had in the Lodge dining hall, a photo of a woman, a man, and a baby during a far different era of life. *Where were those people now? Why weren't they the ones charging through the automatic doors of the hospital, all fuzzy with fear?*

As though he sensed her alarm, Rex chose this moment to call her. She immediately ended it, which was something she would probably regret later. Maybe he thought she wanted out of the marriage already. Maybe some parts of her were so horrified at her body's lack of ability to create a baby, that they actually did want out.

The Emergency Waiting Room was an affront to every single sense. It was crowded and chaotic, packed with tourists who'd had some kind of accident or had gotten sick. A baby screeched in the corner as his mother bobbed him, her cheeks blotchy with fear. An eight-year-old boy held onto his wrist as the rest of his face morphed with pain. His father screamed at someone on the phone as he paced to and fro.

"I hate it here," Alyssa muttered under her breath as she sidled up alongside Maggie.

"Let me just ask about Linda," Maggie said.

Perhaps it should have been expected that the front desk nurse told her it was too soon to know anything about the newest patient. Maggie explained that the woman was her grandmother and that they'd been at the Christmas Market together when she'd collapsed. The nurse told her to sit and to wait along with the others. "We'll let you know when we know more," she explained, almost flippantly. It was clear there was so much on her mind.

Mallory hovered next to the coffee machine and pushed the plastic buttons to make herself a very sweet latte. She passed it off to Maggie, who sipped it as her eyesight grew fuzzy. Alyssa texted someone furiously, probably complaining about Maggie. Mallory heaved a sigh as she lifted her phone, which read LUCAS.

"Hold strong," Maggie told her. "No matter how many insults he hurls at you. You know what you want, now."

Mallory nodded firmly. "And as much as it breaks my heart to say it, it isn't him. It can't be him."

As Alyssa hustled off to the bathroom and Mallory headed outside to speak with Lucas on the phone, Maggie curled herself into a ball on a plastic chair and let out a sob. In a way, she felt she was in the emergency waiting room for another reason— for herself. There was this terrible possibility of a much-older, much-sadder Maggie Potter, without a daughter or a son in sight to care for her, who'd also done something as horrible as collapsing at a Christmas Market alone.

REX: I'm worried about you. Can you call me back?

Maggie shoved her phone back into her pocket and tucked her hair behind her ear. As the baby in the corner let out another wild shriek, she practiced the words she needed to say to Rex. *"I can't have children. I feel completely incomplete as a woman. You married the wrong girl." Would that do? Was it overdramatic? Would Rex suggest adoption? Would she end up hating him for it?*

About an hour later, the nurse at the reception desk greeted her to say that Linda had been treated and would be released. "The situation wasn't so dire that we need to keep her overnight," she explained firmly. "I hope you can bring her safely home?"

Maggie spun round to give Mallory and Alyssa a strained smile. "Of course," she said to the nurse. "We can bring her home."

Maggie hustled after the nurse, whose tennis shoes squeaked across the linoleum floor. They walked down the halls toward the furthest doorway. Once there, Maggie found herself face-to-face with Linda, who was fully dressed and seated in a wheelchair. Her cheeks glowed the slightest bit of pink, and her hands were folded formally across her lap. She looked more like a child just then, rather than a sixty-five-year-old woman.

"Hello..." Linda's voice hummed with curiosity. "They told me my granddaughter was coming to pick me up."

Maggie tried on a slight smile. "That's right. You ready to go?"

Linda turned her eyes to the ground. The nurse instructed her on how to care for herself to ensure something like this never happened again. Maggie stepped around the back of the wheel-chair and adjusted her hands over the handles. When the nurse departed, Linda's shoulders fell forward.

"Another panic attack," she said. "I feel like such a fool."

"I don't think you should feel like a fool," Maggie told her softly. "The world is a terrible place, sometimes. It's a wonder that we aren't all having panic attacks every few minutes."

Linda laughed appreciatively. Maggie began to wheel her down the hall. A nurse burst out from a far-off doorway and hustled toward an emergency. Maggie was so grateful that the emergency wasn't theirs.

"You know, you're the only person I've told about not being able to have kids," Maggie murmured. "Not my sister or my mother or my husband. Just you. When I saw you collapse at the market, I panicked."

Linda turned her head to catch Maggie's eye. "You must have been my guardian angel."

Maggie shrugged. "I don't know. I don't feel up to caring for anyone right now."

"I understand that." Linda set her chin upon her chest. "I know how heavy a secret like that can feel. And I am grateful that you've trusted me with your secret. If you'd like to talk about it, in any respect at all, know that I'm just up at the Lodge. Even if I'm not your real grandmother, I could be your friend."

"I'd like that very much."

Chapter Twelve

Janine wasn't entirely pleased about the news that one of her patients had had a panic attack at a Christmas Market. She bristled at the news, packed up her bag, and headed off to the Lodge immediately, as Maggie, Mallory, and Alyssa sat, exhausted, around the kitchen table, hardly sipping their glasses of wine. Lucas had dropped off Zachery a half-hour before and he now slept in his crib upstairs. The baby monitor remained quiet on the table between them, a forever link to that angel upstairs.

"Your mother is very passionate about her work," Grandma Nancy affirmed as she joined them at the table. "It's the first time I can think of since she's been with us at the Lodge that one of our own ended up at the hospital. I'm sure she's panicked."

Alyssa and Mallory went to bed a half-hour before Janine's arrival home. Maggie remained slumped at the kitchen table, her head heavy with anxious thoughts. Janine poured herself a glass of wine and sat across from her as her eyelids drooped.

"She seems okay," Janine offered finally. "Just exhausted. I don't think she followed the protocol I laid out for her. When I spoke with her yesterday, she seemed so focused. So ready to change and become... better. I don't know what happened."

Maggie heaved a sigh. "She seems like the loneliest woman I've met in my life."

Janine pressed a hand over her forehead. Her eyes met Maggie's and held onto them. Just when Maggie thought she might find the strength to tell her mother the heavy thoughts on her mind, there was a soft knock at the front door. Janine bucked back so that the kitchen chair shrieked over the hardwood of the kitchen floor.

"That's Henry," she whispered. "He said he'd stop by tonight."

Maggie nodded, both disappointed and not that she hadn't had the chance to confess. "He's good to you."

"Maybe more than I deserve," Janine countered with a small smile before she headed through the living room toward the foyer. There was the slight screech of the door before their muffled greetings. Maggie sipped the rest of her wine alone and studied the darkness outside the window. Some fifty feet away was the edge of the ocean, its frothy mouth lapping up across the sands. She forced herself to grab her phone and text Rex back with some sort of explanation.

MAGGIE: Hi, honey! I'm sorry about earlier. Things have been really weird today. One of Mom's patients had a health emergency and I spent some time in the ER, waiting to make sure she was okay.

MAGGIE: I'll be back in the city in a few days. I forgot

that I agreed to an interview with the Calamity Art Gallery. Do you think I have it in me to be a curator?

Rex read and responded almost immediately.

REX: I wondered if you ever heard back from them!

REX: Congratulations on the interview. It'll be great to have you back. The apartment has felt really big and empty without you. (I guess we'll think it's way too small when we have our first baby, lol, so I should be soaking up this feeling.)

There he went again: building familiarity and good humor with Maggie, who yearned to resist it at every corner. Her stomach ached. It was her own fault. She hadn't told him anything. He remained in the dark.

REX: Let me make you dinner so we can catch up at home! I don't want to share you with any other city folks. Just you and me and as much pasta as we can eat. Deal?

Maggie didn't respond. Tomorrow, she would write him that she'd accidentally fallen asleep before texting back. Instead, she walked up to the bedroom she shared with Alyssa and slipped beneath the sheets, not bothering to scrub her face of makeup. The two-hundred-dollar night cream she'd purchased for her face remained unused. Something about life just then seemed inappropriate to preserve. Let the wrinkles form. Let the skin dry out.

The following morning, Alyssa spread peanut butter over a slice of bread as Maggie hovered nearby with a coffee mug lifted to her mouth. She'd told Alyssa about the potential curator position at the Brooklyn-based art gallery, and Alyssa had begun a seemingly forever-long rant about the people she knew who'd featured their art at that very gallery and whether or not they were any good. Alyssa was often very judgmental, without the know-how to back it up. This was sometimes loveable and sometimes not.

"But what are you going to wear to the interview?" Alyssa demanded now as she lifted her peanut butter-laden bread to her teeth.

"Gosh, I don't know." Maggie sipped her coffee. "Maybe I won't go at all."

"What? Are you insane? You've wanted a position like this for ages," Alyssa countered. She then tossed her sleep-mussed hair and said, "I know things are weird right now Mags. But you'd regret it if you didn't at least attend the interview. Dad can't screw up every other thing in our lives just because he decided to go and die on us."

That afternoon, Alyssa headed off to visit their cousin, Cole, which left Maggie with hours of in-her-head time. Her thoughts soon turned tumultuous. She found herself on a long walk along the water's edge, headed straight for the Lodge. Once on the outskirts of the Lodge's property, she drummed up the strength to head inside and inquire about Linda. She prayed she was still around.

"She's still here," Mallory assured her from the front desk. "I'm sure she would love to see you. Let me call her room..." Mallory dialed the bedroom extension. Soft rings came through the speaker of the front desk phone before Linda's answer. When Mallory hung up, she nodded and said, "She said she just had a nap and would love a visit."

Maggie headed up to Linda's bedroom, which was the smallest in the Lodge and, therefore, the one often left abandoned. The door was slightly cracked, and the sound of classical music trickled out into the hall. Maggie rapped her knuckles gently across the wood. Linda popped up on the other side of the door and delivered a sterling smile.

"This is a surprise!"

Maggie hovered outside the door, unsure of what to do. Something told her to hug this woman; another part of her insisted it was a boundary she shouldn't cross.

"My mom said she came up to see you yesterday?"

Linda's eyes clouded. "She did. She's such a sweet woman. She gave me a little lecture about taking care of myself." She laughed dryly. "I can't say I don't deserve lectures and harsh words. I do."

"You deserve to take care of yourself," Maggie breathed.

Again, silence brewed between them. Maggie's heart drummed ominously.

"Do you want to go for a drive?" Maggie finally asked.

Linda cocked her head. "That doesn't sound too bad."

"Let me just see if we can borrow Mallory's car," Maggie said. "I'm sure she won't mind."

Fifteen minutes later, Maggie found herself in the front seat of Mallory's car with Linda buckled in tightly beside her. Linda wore a thick pair of sunglasses, even against the strange grey light of the day. Maggie pressed harder on the gas and sped them westward, away from Edgartown and the Lodge and out toward the craggy cliffside of Aquinnah. When they first spotted the glorious edge of the island, Linda gasped inwardly.

"I haven't seen anything so beautiful in years," she whispered.

Maggie parked the car at the edge of the cliffside, in full view of the newly-built-up Aquinnah Cliffside Overlook Hotel, which would reopen the following summer after nearly eighty years of closure after a colossal hurricane had ripped across the island. She explained what she knew of the story to Linda, who shook her head ominously.

"It's amazing how much history this island seems to have," Linda whispered. "Sometimes I think that's my biggest worry about my own life, that my history won't be known by anyone and that I'll just end up alone and afraid and without context."

Maggie's throat tightened. "I've felt the same since I found out about my depressing diagnosis." She closed her eyes as a shudder overtook her. "I hope it's okay that I ask you this. It's been heavy on my mind."

"Okay," Linda murmured.

Maggie gave her a sideway glance. "That baby in the photograph and that man. Who are they?"

And why aren't they here with you? She wanted to ask it. The words burned at the edge of her tongue.

Linda groaned. "I don't know. What is there to say? I used to have a very different life. It all slipped through my fingers. It feels more like a dream now than anything I could have ever known."

Maggie's disappointment at the response was sharp. At this moment, a forceful wind swept in from the Atlantic and made the car creak around them.

"Why can't you be honest? Really, really honest?" Maggie breathed as the creaking subsided.

Linda shook her head. "I don't know how to trust anyone anymore. It's been so long."

"But I'm asking because... because I do care..." Maggie whispered.

"I don't know. All I know is that I was very, very selfish when I was younger. Maybe even now," Linda continued. "I see how everyone else wears their selfishness. It's protection. I feel that I can't trust anyone to hold my story properly, so I have to keep it safe. I have to keep it..."

Maggie swallowed. "I don't want to be selfish. I want to help you carry your secret, the way you've carried mine."

Again, silence fell between them. Linda swept a hand over her cheek. Perhaps she'd forgotten how to tell her own story. Perhaps she'd lost the words.

But finally, she spoke.

"I fell in love exactly once in my life," she began. "I was a twenty-something on a seemingly never-ending trek of adventures. But this man made me rethink everything. I stopped traveling. I stopped thinking about my stupid, stubborn belief that I wanted to see the entire world. I found myself in a kind of prison in Paris — in love yet not fully understanding what love truly meant."

Maggie felt the words like a gift. She turned to face this sixty-five-year-old woman, a woman who'd loved and lost. It was difficult to imagine her as a twenty-something in Paris. Perhaps when Maggie turned sixty-five, too, it would be difficult for those around her to imagine her the way she was now. How strange time was.

"Is that the man you had the baby with?" Maggie asked softly.

Linda dropped her eyelashes over her cheeks. In the distance, the construction railed on for the Aquinnah Cliffside Overlook Hotel. The sounds echoed out across the Vineyard Sound.

"Happiness is a choice, I think," Linda whispered then. "And I've often felt that I never understood how to make that choice, even when it was right there in front of me."

Maggie understood that Linda had told her all she could for the time being. As the snow began to curl out from the skies above, she started the engine and drove them back toward the

Lodge. Once outside, Linda gave her a limp-armed hug and turned back into the warmth that awaited her.

"Promise you'll take care of yourself?" Maggie called, just before Linda headed into the Lodge.

Linda pretended not to hear. The door clicked closed behind her and left Maggie alone beneath the soft flakes of snow.

Chapter Thirteen

The interview for Calamity Art Gallery took place at two-thirty in the afternoon. Maggie arrived back in the city that morning, armed with intellectually stimulating conversation topics about the art world and a real "eye" for how the gallery's future could go. No, her heart wasn't in it, not in the slightest. But maybe in life, you had to "fake it till you make it." It was an expression for a reason.

Rex texted her, *"good luck"* and also a *"can't wait to see you tonight and hear all about it."* Maggie was grateful to be at the apartment they'd shared for years alone. Rex had kept it fairly tidy, although there was a large pile of unwashed laundry on the bathroom floor and several socks on the couch. The place smelled of both of them and a number of her items were admittedly strewn across the counter, still. Probably, they'd acted as a constant reminder for Rex that she wasn't around, that she'd left without explanation. Her stomach tightened with guilt.

Maggie dressed in a trendy blazer and a pair of tight-fitting pants along with a pair of black Louboutins. It was funny to dress city-chic after over a week on the island. She had lived out much of her time in only sweatpants. Her city friends wouldn't have recognized her.

The interview for curator of Calamity Art Gallery went just about as good as any interview could have. Maggie spoke eloquently about her art opinions and the direction she wanted to take the space. The three board members, two of which wore very trendy, thick eye frames, seemed impressed. Toward the end of the interview, however, the middle-aged woman at the table said, "We realize you just got married. It's not politically correct for us to ask this, but it's essential to our planning, as we don't like to waste time. Any plans on getting pregnant soon?"

Maggie gave off no indication that the question bothered her, even as it sliced through her like a samurai sword.

"No plans at all," she told them primly.

Maggie returned home just in time to burst into tears in the bathroom. She stood beneath the scalding hot shower and curved her shoulders forward as the steam grew thicker within the small space. The bathroom's tub was a glorious antique-like bathtub, a gift from Rex. Probably, he hadn't envisioned her weeping about their inability to have children in that very tub.

Maggie wrapped herself up in a robe and brushed her teeth. Her mind was extremely heavy, and her limbs ached to lay out across the expensive mattress Rex's parents had purchased them for their wedding present. When she opened the bathroom door to allow the steam to escape, however, she heard the clattering of Rex in the kitchen. Her heart seized with fear.

"There she is!" Rex hustled down the hallway, still in his business suit, his tie on either side of his shoulders. His eyes glowed with love for her, despite her soaking wet hair and her robe. He pressed a kiss on her lips, even as she stewed with the realization that actually, she didn't feel she deserved his love.

She'd hidden away from him. She had lied to him. And now, he'd welcomed her back with the beginnings of a home-cooked meal and a warm kiss.

"Hi," she finally forced herself to say.

"I missed you! You're back!"

Maggie heard herself laugh. Perhaps this would have been a silly moment had she been in a better mood. She pointed toward the bedroom and said, "Just let me get dressed and then I'll join you."

"Why get dressed?" Rex teased as he tugged at the tie of her robe. "Just a waste of time."

Maggie dropped her eyes to the ground. Immediately, the mood between them shifted. Rex stepped back.

"What's wrong, Maggie?" His tone was sharp and deep. He'd seen the depth of her eyes. He'd recognized just how little she wanted to be intimate with him, especially now. "Did the interview go badly?"

"No. It went well," Maggie replied softly. "They said they're going to let me know within the week, but I have a feeling I got it."

Rex's smile was confused. "Congratulations. That's incredible." He skipped a beat, then added, "Come on. Come to the kitchen. Let me pour you a glass of wine to celebrate."

Maggie shook her head softly even as she allowed him to lead her to the kitchen. He had purchased a very expensive bottle of wine, which now breathed on the counter. Everything in their lives was expensive. Would it ever be enough to fill the hole in her heart? He poured them both glasses and lifted his toward the light.

"Here's to your next chapter," Rex said firmly. "I can't wait to watch you as you take this on with ease."

Maggie clinked her glass with his as she stewed with inner resentment. Why did she feel this way toward the man she loved so much? Why couldn't she just fall into his arms and cry?

"How's the island these days?" Rex asked finally. He placed the glass of wine down on the counter and began to hunt for the cutting board and pots and pans for his home-cooked pasta recipe.

"Oh, fine." Maggie placed her elbow on the counter. "Alyssa is just as dramatic as ever. Mallory and Lucas officially broke up."

"That's too bad," Rex murmured.

"I mean, not really," Maggie countered. "Lucas has been nothing but a child the past few months. His tantrums got in the way of Mallory's happiness."

"Yeah, but..." Rex shifted his weight. "I was pulling for them. They're a family."

Maggie's heart nearly exploded with sorrow. Had she wanted Mallory and Lucas to break up just so others would be as miserable as she felt?

"Not everything can work out, Rex," Maggie informed him flippantly.

Rex's eyes looked wounded. He set a pan on the counter with a clank. After a long moment of silence, he asked, "Why do I feel like you're talking about us rather than Mallory and Lucas?"

Maggie's lips parted in surprise. Rex had always been able to read her. *Why had she assumed she could hide all this away?* Tears sprung to her eyes. Rex's eyes almost immediately matched hers.

Gosh, what was wrong with her? This man wasn't Lucas. He was powerful and alive and wild with love for her. Sure, he'd missed the most important doctor's appointment of her life, but worse than that, she had lied to him about the results. What a mess it all was.

"Just tell me, Maggie," Rex breathed as he closed his eyes. "Tell me if you regret marrying me. Tell me if you want to separate for a while. I can take it. Really."

Somehow, hearing Rex verbalize this made it even worse. Tears streaked down her cheek.

"I have only ever loved you, Rex. You're the one," she whispered. She then stepped around the counter and pressed a hand over his chest to feel the fluttering of his anxious heart beneath the fabric of his shirt.

"Then why does it feel like you're so far away from me?" Rex asked.

Maggie blinked rapidly in an attempt to stop her crying. "There's just a lot going on in my head right now. A lot I need to deal with. I suddenly don't know how I want my life to go. Or how I see myself in five years or ten years or…"

Rex sipped his wine. How could Maggie translate everything in her confused, anxious head? Rex had destroyed himself with work the previous few months, all for the extension of their family and the happiness of their future.

"We don't have to have a baby yet," Rex murmured. "We can table that conversation for another time. We're still young. We can travel the world. We can spend our money on trips to Paris and macarons and pairs of shoes."

Maggie's throat tightened. She tried to speak, but nothing spilled out.

"I understand that you want to be a mother soon," Rex breathed. "But if it's too much stress on us, maybe it shouldn't be now."

Maggie's hand curled into a fist. "I don't know what to say."

"Let me just make dinner. Let me just take care of you for once. You've been gone for ages," Rex continued hurriedly. He realized he'd said too much and stepped in it. "Let's just catch up. Tell me more about Alyssa. Tell me about Grandma Nancy. I want all updates."

But Maggie's fatigue felt insurmountable. How could she possibly sit there with him and pretend that everything was all right? She shook her head and pointed herself toward the bedroom. "I just need to sleep, Rex. I'm sorry."

Maggie made her way to her bedroom and collapsed on her side of the bed. She shivered despite the warmth of her comforter. In no time at all, she slipped into a deep sleep, only to awake an hour later. Rex's strong arm was wrapped around her as he spooned her. His snores were light and tender. She shifted herself deeper into him and inhaled his scent. She hadn't known how much she'd missed him.

Her shifting awakened him and he spoke to her softly.

"You must be so hungry."

Maggie laughed with surprise. She turned around so that her nose touched against his. He kissed her tenderly with his eyes still closed.

"Come on. Let's order pizza," he said.

Maggie's laughter turned to silly giggles. "What are you talking about? We're already in bed."

"Maggie. I don't know what kind of old woman you've turned into, but it's only eight-fifteen," Rex countered. "This was only a mid-evening nap. We've got a big, expensive bottle of wine to drink, and I'm famished. You can cry as much as you want, but I'm feeding you no matter what you say. Is that clear?"

Maggie's smile couldn't be helped. Her love for him ballooned out from her. Soon, she would tell him everything, but just then, she wanted to live in the cocoon of his love.

"It's crystal clear," she told him before she kissed his nose again. "Can we get extra cheese pizza? With cheesy crust?"

Rex rolled his eyes, feigning annoyance. "You've got to be kidding me. All these demands?"

"I know. I'm terrible," she returned.

Rex stood from the bed and stretched his arms skyward. The grey light from outside curled over his muscular form. Maggie couldn't help but visualize them in another reality, rising in the dark to care for their baby. This wasn't their season of life. This season was a season of waiting. It was a season of love and attempts at understanding. It was all it could be.

Chapter Fourteen

"You're going to have to try to work with me here, Linda. I want to help you. And you want help, don't you? Isn't that why you came all the way here from the city? Isn't that why we're in this office right now?"

Dr. Janine Grimson Potter scowled over her eyeglasses at Linda, who sat in the Lodge-given robe with her ankles crossed and her eyes to the corner. In the wake of her panic attack at the Christmas Market, Dr. Janine had set aside a number of minutes per day to speak exclusively to Linda. Linda sensed that this made the rest of Janine's schedule off-kilter, as she had several other patients. Her eyes burned with worry for Linda. It was unlike anything Linda had ever seen before, save for Janine's own daughter's eyes. Why had that girl followed her to the hospital like that? Why had she even remembered Linda's name? The questions seemed outside of time and space.

"Come on, Linda. Can you even hear me?" Janine asked. "I've never personally sent someone to a psychiatry facility after the

Lodge, but I'm not afraid to do it if I feel my patient is in an espe-cially dire situation. Please. Talk to me."

"I just thought maybe I would be different here," Linda finally answered as her throat tightened. "I thought I would feel..." She trailed off as her eyes dropped to the ground.

Janine scribbled something onto her pad of paper. It seemed that she'd scrawled over one hundred things when seated across from Linda. Almost assuredly, she was no closer to compre-hending the strangeness within Linda's mind than Linda was.

"Have you considered meeting with a therapist to discuss your panic attacks?" Janine asked in almost a whisper.

"I don't have health insurance. It makes it a bit difficult," Linda countered.

Janine nodded. Linda sensed the other question, which hung in the air: how in the heck had Linda paid for this session at the Lodge if she couldn't even get herself into proper therapy? That was a very complicated question with an even more complicated answer.

"Did you ever have health insurance?" Janine tried.

Linda opted for the truth, just to see where it landed. "I've never had it in the States. I gave birth abroad. They don't take an arm and a leg from you for a hospital stay. In fact, they allowed me and my baby to stay around for three, no, four days, and it was free."

Janine grimaced. "Our health system is quite difficult here in the States. I'll give you that." Her face echoed her exasperation. She looked as though she wanted to inquire more about this "baby" that Linda had had abroad, but she soon clamped her lips together and blinked up at the clock. "I hate to do this, but I have to move on to the next patient. I know you're here a few more days. I hope during that time, you'll find a way to open up to me a bit more. I want to help you, Linda. I want to find a way through the pain you're experiencing. I believe that everyone has the ability to find peace. It just takes time and a lot, a lot of work."

Linda returned to her bedroom, where she sat at the edge of her bed and swung her thin legs out in front of her. Janine represented so much to Linda— namely, the act of building a story of your life that had several different acts with several different periods of growth. Linda had had just a brief time of happiness, followed by the act of running away from her problems for decades at a time. What was depression, if not escapism? What was her inability to connect, if not her refusal to allow anyone on the planet to know her?

Linda hunted for her old journal, which she'd lodged into the back of her backpack. Once she lifted it, she avoided all signs of that old photograph, as it seemed almost poisonous. Midway through the notebook, she paused to read some of the entries, scribed by a far different version of Linda, who had lived a far different version of the one she led now.

April 17, 1979

I suppose I was foolish to think that the love was the sort that would sustain me for the rest of my days. It stands to reason that I lived in my head like this— that I thought, after all that hardship back in New York City, I was the sort of woman special enough to fall head-over-heels with a Frenchman and live happily ever after. What kind of nonsense is that?

Our baby is now two years old (no longer a baby, I suppose).

She babbles in French and lifts her beautiful eyes to us with joy and assurance. She doesn't know that her father sometimes leaves at night for hours and hours at a time, without a word for when he'll return. She doesn't know that I built my whole life on the belief of his lies.

My depression was always something I carried around as a little kid. I cried in school corners and on buses and benches. I cried for hours once in Central Park when I was convinced my mother had forgotten to pick me up. In reality, she thought I was having too good of a time with friends— something that, I can assure anyone, never happened.

I thought he was the one. I thought our baby had solidified this truth.

Yet here I am in Paris. April in Paris. And I feel no closer to happiness nor joy nor knowledge of some greater truth.

It was painful to read these words. Linda swiped a hand over her forehead as the memories came back to her. She felt the crippling reality of this woman's world. She felt the sorrow, without any of the anger that she maybe should have had. Only a month or so later, she discovered that her husband was having an affair. He'd shrugged it off, saying that this was what Frenchmen did. As an American, this was difficult for Linda to fully grasp. She found herself thinking of herself as a prude. Why couldn't she get on board with the French sensibilities, if only for their baby?

Her depression grew worse. She could feel it in the words on the pages as she continued forward.

December 25, 1979

He looked like he wanted to beat me today.

Does he beat the woman he's seeing?

Does the fact that he didn't beat me matter? Or does the sheer fact that he wanted to obliterate all other facts?

I never wanted to be my mother. I wanted to have an exciting, beautiful life.

It's Christmas. My French is fine, good sometimes, actually, and I find myself willfully chatting with strangers, just for someone else to connect with. He told me over and over again that I don't cook the same way his mother cooks. I would kill someone for an American hamburger.

Will my daughter ever know American soil? Will she ever learn to speak English the way I want her to?

Will I have the strength, one day, to take her away from her father and build us a new life?

I can hardly keep myself alive. I don't know if...

That's a question for another day. Not today. Not Christmas.

Linda had finally found the strength to leave her marriage when her daughter was four years old. The year was 1981, and Linda was at the end of her rope, both physically and mentally. Strain from her husband's horrendous words and hope that he would someday return to her romantically had kept her from eating a proper meal for many years. She'd grown skeletal and listless. Her daughter had sometimes cried for many minutes before Linda could fully hear her. It was as though she existed in another world.

Where had she gone after that? She wasn't sure any longer. Had the next job been in China? England? Portugal? She flipped through the pages of her journal to find that she hadn't bothered to write any of her life happenings for several months after her departure. Leaving her daughter in France had cut her in two. She couldn't care for herself. She had no money and no home. For better or worse, her husband loved their daughter and would ensure she was well-taken care of. Linda was better out of the picture. She didn't want her daughter to have her as a role model. She could hardly even look at herself in the mirror.

Linda had been heartbroken since the year 1981. Since then, she'd had no contact at all with her husband, whom she'd never fully divorced. She sensed that her daughter had no recollection of her whatsoever. What did anyone remember before the age of four? Beyond that, she was half-certain that her husband had filled her daughter's head with horrific stories about Linda, the mother who'd left.

Linda had lived with the ghost of her husband and daughter. She carried them with her, heavily, upon her shoulders. She'd allowed no other form of romance; she'd allowed herself no other feeling of maternal instinct. Since then, she'd been on the run.

Until now.

But what did now mean, anyway? She'd found the Lodge. She'd found something she wanted to cling to. But her body and mind both seemed beyond repair, so much so that when the beautiful and kind and professional Janine Grimson Potter asked her to open up, she resisted. She was like a stone.

Linda thought again about Janine's daughter and what she'd

said about honesty. Linda was terrified of the truth because it seemed to pinpoint her as the villain in her own story. She had left her marriage. She had left her four-year-old daughter. And as a result, she had punished herself each and every day since—without reprieve and without a second thought.

Chapter Fifteen

Maggie's eyelashes fluttered open as new light crept through the cream-colored curtains of the master bedroom. It was a remarkable thing to awaken back in Brooklyn, rather than Martha's Vineyard, and outside, horns beeped wildly as traffic peppered its way through the morning. She cooed inwardly and turned around, hoping to discover Rex beside her. Instead, the space where his body had been was indented but no longer warm, as though he'd been up for a while. A glance at the bedside clock told her: it was just past eight-thirty.

Maggie stepped lightly off the bed and tip-toed in just her dressing gown to the hallway. From there, she heard an abrupt crash, as though Rex hunted for something. She rushed to help him, only to discover that he yanked a suitcase out of the hall closet with the strength of a man who'd gotten "almost too ripped" for their wedding.

"What are you doing?" The sight of him getting out his suitcase made her heart stop beating. Her voice was fraught.

He turned back and grimaced as though surprised that she'd awakened. He had showered already and wore a button-up shirt and a pair of slacks. He raked a hand through his hair and said, "Hey, Mags."

Maggie sensed a rat from a mile away. She crossed her arms over her chest and leaned against the wall. There was a great distance between them, suddenly, as though the script had changed and she hadn't gotten the edits.

"I couldn't sleep last night," Rex told her finally. His voice sounded stern and sterile. "I got to thinking. I was thinking about how you left and wouldn't come back—thinking about how you're keeping something from me— something big. And they asked me to go on a business trip this morning, so I said yes. I need to get away from whatever this is. It isn't healthy for either of us."

Maggie pressed her lips together tightly as her eyes filled with tears.

"I'm no idiot, Mags. I don't know why you're lying to me for the first time in our relationship, but I know I don't like it. I just know that it feels like there is a Grand Canyon between us. And no matter how long I hold you, no matter how many texts I send to you to reach out, no matter how many times I ask you to come home, you'll stay over on your side of the Grand Canyon until you decide differently. It makes me sick, Mags. It makes me sick to feel like I'm looking over at a stranger."

Maggie shook her head violently. "Rex... Please. Please, don't go. Please, I'm back..."

"I didn't marry you to live amongst lies and deceit," he told her firmly. "I married you so that we could be life partners. I married you so that we could make every decision together. But a few weeks ago, you up and just left without any explanation. You wouldn't answer me when I asked you how you were. You hardly treated me like a human, Mags, let alone the man you're supposed to love."

Maggie dropped her chin to her chest as a sob escaped her lips. She had never even considered the possibility that he wouldn't want to be with her any longer. She'd always assumed he would be right there, pestering her with text messages, cradling her as she slept. Here, he stood up to her pain and demanded answers.

And maybe this was what she needed.

Maybe this was what she'd been waiting for.

Maybe this was proof that she didn't have to live this all alone.

"Rex..." Maggie wiped her fingers over her cheek as she drummed up the courage to tell him. She couldn't waste the beautiful world they'd created together.

She couldn't be like Linda described herself— sad and alone and filled with regrets. Sometimes, you had to act. This was one of those times.

"Maggie, please. Tell me." His eyes were the size of saucers. He dropped the suitcase on the floor between them. It would only be filled if she allowed it to be filled.

Finally, Maggie burst into tears. Her shoulders shook as she collapsed in a heap. In a flash, Rex had his arms around her as he whispered, his voice a rasp, "Maggie. Whatever it is, you don't have to deal with this alone. Come on. Talk to me. Please." His lips were warm as he placed little kisses along her jawline, over her eyebrow.

Maggie took a slow, staggered breath. This was it. This was the time she needed to take. The stage was hers.

"That day, you were supposed to meet me at the clinic..." she began.

Rex dropped his shoulders forward. "I know, baby. I'm so sorry I missed it. I hate myself for it. It feels like everything changed that day."

Maggie shook her head vehemently. "It did. When you asked me what happened at the clinic, I lied to you."

Rex shifted his head up. His eyes met hers. Maggie remembered, with startling accuracy, what it had felt like to gaze into those eyes and pledge her life forever. Things had felt so different then. Her dream of being a mother naturally had remained within her. Her father had sat in the audience, alive and just as mean as ever.

"I found out that I can't have children naturally," Maggie rasped.

Rex's lips parted in surprise. "But you're only twenty-five…"

Maggie furrowed her brow as Rex hurriedly apologized.

"I'm sorry. I'm sorry. I'm listening," he whispered.

Maggie cleared her throat and explained everything she now knew about her health and that the likelihood of getting pregnant on her own, or even at all, was very low. Rex listened as his eyes widened with surprise. She could feel his hesitation in everything he did. After all, wasn't Maggie healthy? Wasn't she almost next to perfect? They'd always thought so before. They would never think so again.

When Maggie finished her story, Rex dug his face into her shoulder and held onto her as tightly as he could in a way that made her feel wholly protected. She remained in his embrace for what seemed like a small eternity before he stood and helped her to her feet.

"Don't you need to go on your business trip?" Maggie whispered.

"Don't be stupid, Mags," Rex told her point-blank. "I'm not going anywhere."

Rex led her back to bed, where he tucked her beneath the sheets before retreating into the hallway to call his boss about his inability to fly away from the city. He called it a "family emergency." As Maggie listened to the familiar sound of Rex's voice, she found herself falling back into sleep. Her eyelids danced low and darkness crept over her.

When she awoke several hours later, she found Rex scooped up behind her, cradling her warmly and lovingly. She turned into him and repositioned her head on the pillow, the one they'd picked out together for their wedding registry. Their lives were weaved together in nearly every way. Why had she thought she wanted any other world but this one?

"I'm glad you didn't go," she whispered.

"No. I already messed up bad when I missed that horrible doctor's appointment." Rex shook his head with shame and then added, "I'll never miss anything like that again. You shouldn't have to carry that weight alone."

Maggie furrowed her brow. "I shouldn't have made such a big deal about it. Your career is important. And neither of us knew just how bad it would be."

Rex buzzed his lips. "You're my number one. You're it for me, Mags. And..." He closed his eyes for a long moment, then continued. "If you feel up to it, I've been reading about IVF this morning. It's a big undertaking. It can take a lot out of us. I know that. But if you feel up to it..."

The mere fact that he had spent time researching a potential resolve for them to have a baby together filled Maggie's heart with hope and longing. It showed the true depths of his love for her and she was grateful for it.

"I'll probably be crazy with hormones," she whispered. "I'll probably eat all of the candy in the house and then send you out for more. I'll probably yell and scream and cry and laugh all in the span of five minutes."

"And that's so different from normal, how?" Rex teased.

Maggie erupted with laughter. The giggles made her stomach bounce as she tossed herself onto her back and stared at the ceiling. What a perfect man! What a perfect father he would be! What a less-than-perfect start to something great!

"I already called the doctor's office. The one in Manhattan," Rex said softly. "And they said there's an appointment tomorrow to begin the entire process. But if you're up for it..."

Maggie spun into him and wrapped her arms around him as tight as she could. The thwack-thwack of his beating heart made her body quake.

"Does that mean we're headed to our first IVF appointment tomorrow?" Rex asked.

Maggie laughed. "Yes. It does."

Rex laced his fingers through hers and gazed at her lovingly. For the first time, they operated as a team, just as they'd pledged to do mere months ago. This had been an initial hiccup. But through this hardship, Maggie had discovered a great deal about herself, about life, and about how harrowing it could become if you weren't brave enough to face it head-on. She was ready— ready for treatments, the unbalanced hormones, and the upcoming disappointments, only to try everything all over again. With Rex by her side, she could do anything. She finally recognized that about herself, now. He was her missing link.

Chapter Sixteen

With the truth shared with Rex, Maggie now found a sincere solace and peace, one that allowed her to laugh and joke and converse in ways she'd thought were now impossible. It was a funny thing about grief; at some point, it just became something you carried along with you as you found new ways to become yourself. As the morning drifted toward afternoon, she and Rex showered and changed into hip Brooklyn fashion and set out on the streets for something to eat. Maggie's fingers slipped evenly through Rex's as they bustled through Bushwick before eventually stumbling into a little brunch place. Every inch of the space was decorated with Christmas, with three Christmas trees in three different corners, mistletoe low on the wooden ceiling beams, and glittering tinsel. Christmas tunes buzzed out from the speakers. Maggie placed her head tenderly on Rex's chest as they waited to be seated.

"I have a real taste for Bloody Marys today," Rex informed her as they sat across from one another and held hands across the table.

"Me too," Maggie returned brightly. She glanced out toward the window that stretched across the room, offering a glorious view of a snow-capped Brooklyn. A young girl in an overly large, fluffed blue hat swept past, her thin legs whipping out in front of her. Two boys chased after her, and their laughter rang out across the windows and through the crack in the door.

When Maggie returned her eyes to Rex's, he grinned sheepishly and said, "I've started to think about our kids growing up here, too."

Maggie laughed. "If my dad knew I wanted to raise my children in Brooklyn, he wouldn't know what to say."

"We're going to make our own way," Rex offered. "We'll have children however we can. And we'll raise them however we like."

Maggie lifted her chin. "Summers on the Vineyard with Mom and Henry?"

"I don't see why not," Rex affirmed.

They ordered a beautiful selection of Bloody Marys and yogurts and breakfast sandwiches with goopy yellow eggs, crispy bacon, and melted cheese from the waitress. The conversation seemed unbridled, especially now, and Maggie found herself asking Rex questions she never had.

"What kind of father do you think you'll be?"

Rex considered this for a moment. He tapped his napkin over his lips as the grey light from the street glittered in his eyes. Maggie was proud of herself for saying "will be" rather than "would you be." They now operated in the assurance that it was their future.

"I want to be a silly father," he said, surprising Maggie so much that she burst into laughter. "Let me finish," he continued with a smile. "I want to be silly, you know, the kind with all the best dad jokes. But I also want to be kind and considerate and strong of will. I want to keep my word. I don't want to miss anything, not a kindergarten graduation or a dance recital or a trip to the Vineyard. I want to be there for their first steps and their first words. I want it all."

Their Bloody Marys arrived. Rex poked his straw through the thick red liquid and shrugged. "Ever since you went away..."

"Gosh, Rex, I'm so sorry..."

He met her gaze and shook his head. "I don't mean to make you feel guilty. I just want to say that ever since you went away, I've had all these dreams about fatherhood. I think a part of me feared that I wouldn't be able to have that life with you, the woman I've longed to build a life with since we met."

Maggie sipped her Bloody Mary as images of Rex as a father flowed through her mind.

"I can't believe we're going to be allowed to see so many things together. So many experiences. So many hardships. So many beautiful views and moments..." she began.

Rex nodded. "Old age isn't anything you think about when you meet and have a few drunken dates."

"And then suddenly, you find yourself in your mid-twenties, with a messed-up uterus and a strange will to eat kale, if only, so it'll make you live a little bit longer," Maggie said with a wry smile. "And you start to consider what it might be like to be thirty-five or forty-five or even my grandmother's age. Grandma Nancy made countless mistakes, but look at her now. She fell in love with her soulmate. She now runs his Lodge and is best friends with his daughters."

Their breakfast sandwiches arrived. Maggie took a fork and

knife to hers, slashing through the yolk so that yellow pooled across the right-hand side of the plate. Rex took his in his hands and took a large bite, which cast yolk down his chin instead. Maggie laughed outright as he tidied himself.

"You'll be looking at this guy getting egg all over his face for the rest of your life!" Rex chuckled and tossed his head back.

After they calmed down, Maggie told Rex a bit about Linda, the older woman at the Lodge whom she'd grown closer to over the previous few weeks. "I worry about women like that. Women who have no love to speak of. I try to imagine what it's like to get up in the morning. On my darkest days, I knew, always, that you or Alyssa would pester me to keep going. But there hasn't been anyone around to force Linda forward."

Rex furrowed his brow. "It sounds like she needed you much more than she even realized."

"I need to get her number," Maggie affirmed. "She lives in Manhattan. We could have her over? If she'd be open to that."

"I would love that," Rex replied. He sipped his Bloody Mary, his eyes shadowed with introspection, then said, "Have you thought any more about telling your mother what's going on with you?"

"I know that I need to. Maybe this evening I'll give her a call. Tell her about our plan to do IVF. Tell her how... frightened but excited I am."

Rex nodded. "Might as well be honest about everything now. We're going to need as much support as we can get."

That evening, Maggie situated herself at the edge of her and Rex's king-sized mattress, crossed her legs, and dialed her mother. The phone rang three times before Janine answered in the brightest tone. Even her voice sent Maggie into a mini-reel. After all Janine had been through the previous year, Maggie felt guilty for adding another smattering of darkness. It couldn't be helped. She needed her mother to help carry her.

"Hi, honey," Janine began. "We've missed you here on the Vineyard! How did your job interview go?"

"It went really well, Mom." Maggie's throat tightened. "But that's not why I'm calling." She closed her eyes tightly, then began. "Rex and I went to the doctor a few weeks ago. I sensed there was something off with us— with me. Pregnancy seemed like it should have been instantaneous, but after six months of trying..."

Janine's voice was full of hope. "Oh, honey. They tell you to wait a full year, at least, don't they?"

"It doesn't matter anymore because we know the truth, now. And the truth is, it's going to be a real struggle for us to have kids of our own."

There was silence on the other line. Janine's voice seemed so far away. "Honey, what happened? What is it?"

Maggie explained the best she could about her tilted uterus and her decision to hide the information from the rest of them for the past few weeks, as she hadn't been able to face it herself. "I wanted to live in another reality. I didn't want to face the idea that everything I've always wanted couldn't be mine. But Rex forced me to open up to him, and since then, I've felt much so much better, lighter. We have our first appointment for IVF tomorrow, and I'm looking forward to it. I know that these things don't always take the first or even second time. But I'm hopeful. For the first time since Dad died, I'm hopeful."

Janine let out a single sob and then quickly said, "I'm so sorry, honey. The fact that you had to carry this on your own for any amount of time is a lot to take in. I hate that you felt you couldn't come to me with this."

"I know, Mom. But I had to deal with it in my own time. I can't explain it."

"Alyssa and I will drive to the city tomorrow for your first appointment," Janine affirmed. "I'll cancel my appointments."

At that moment, Rex peeked through the crack in the bedroom doorway. He held a mug of hot chocolate aloft and gave Maggie a soft smile.

"I think Rex and I can handle this on our own," Maggie told her mother as Rex crept closer and passed her the mug.

"Honey, we want to be there for you in any way we can."

"I know that," Maggie murmured. "But you've already done so much just by being there. I had a place to process all of this on the Vineyard. And being surrounded by your love... it helped more than you could even understand."

In the background of the phone call, baby Zachery let out a wild yelp. Maggie's heart lifted. "Is that who I think it is?"

"Mallory and Zachery just got home. Mallory waved to say hi." Janine paused for a long moment, then added, "She told me she's happy she found the strength to officially end things with Lucas. Now, she can move on to the next phase of her life. Whatever that means." Janine paused again before adding, "Gosh, honey. I see now why you were so angry with Lucas."

"I shouldn't have taken it all out on him," Maggie returned. "I just couldn't understand why he handled something so precious without all the love in the world like he is supposed to."

"It's true what they say. You never fully appreciate what you have until you're forced to," Janine offered. "I've thought about that over and over again in so many regards."

"I could see it in your eyes when you made us drive across Spain and Portugal, just so you could tell Henry how much he meant to you," Maggie pointed out.

Janine's laughter was infectious yet tinged with sorrow. "We're all running toward what we think will bring us happiness."

"We're running as fast as we can," Maggie offered as Rex slipped behind her and wrapped his arms around her stomach. "I have to go, Mom. But I'll be back on the island in a few days. I love you so much."

"I love you, too, honey. You'll get through this. You've always gotten through everything else before."

Maggie hung up the phone and placed her head against Rex's chest. The bump-bump of his heart buzzed through her head and shoulders. If she closed her eyes just so, she could imagine them sitting like this, with a baby in her arms. As it was, they were just two young people, in love, seated in the grey haze of an evening in Brooklyn. Christmas came swiftly and with it the promise of beautiful conversations around the Christmas tree, the kind of hugs that made you forget all your pain, for just a split-second, at least, and buckets of food and gut-busting laughter. There was so much to look forward to. If only it was easier to live in the present moments of beauty without longing for some other future.

Chapter Seventeen

"It seems like this is your last weekend with us." Doctor Janine settled into the chair across her office as Linda crossed and uncrossed her ankles beneath her. Doctor Janine's eyes burrowed into Linda's with seemingly endless curiosity. "And I wanted to ask you. What could we here at the Lodge do for you before you go? Is there a way we could make your passage back to the city easier for you? A way we could attack this anxiety and depression head-on and help you cultivate tools to deal with it later on?"

Linda gaped at this beautiful, successful, well-loved creature and felt the heaviness of her empty stomach, the ache of her heart. How could she possibly translate her loneliness into words that Janine Grimson Potter could understand? Had she ever spent an evening alone, wondering if anyone would even notice if she passed on from this world? Had she ever dealt with the immensity of her own mistakes?

"Nothing comes to mind," Linda tried now. She rubbed the terrycloth of her robe and willed herself to come up with something, anything to make poor Janine feel as though she'd helped in some small way.

Janine's shoulders slumped forward. "We've gone over meditation. Nutrition. Exercise. We've discussed the ways stress develops in the body and disallows your full breadth of health. We've…"

Linda cleared her throat distractedly. Her eyes turned toward the door as she willed time to hurry up and get her out of there. She'd given the Lodge a try. Perhaps it was her last good try of her life.

"I'm sorry," Janine said finally, at a loss. "I feel like I failed you. And I hate feeling this way. I wish there was a way we could work together in a better way. I wish…"

Linda lifted her chin and interrupted, grateful she'd found a topic for her tongue to land on. "And how's your daughter? I haven't seen her around lately." Her heart banged with sorrow. "It was so sweet of her to check up on me at the hospital." How could she possibly translate that it was the first realm of kindness she'd experienced in decades?

Janine's lips curved slightly upward with confusion. "Maggie is a very special woman," she replied finally.

"She was curious about me," Linda said finally. "She asked me some questions about myself and my life that nobody ever has."

Janine tilted her head. "I didn't know that."

Linda shrugged. "It made me think about some stuff that I didn't want to think about."

"Sounds like she pushed you."

"She did." Linda's voice cracked. "I was hoping to see her around before I head back to the city."

Janine's eyes dropped to the ground between them. "She should be back very soon." After another pause, she added, "She's been going through hardships of her own. I never imagined that my daughter would want to hide away like that, not from me."

Linda recognized, now, that Maggie had finally confessed the news of her infertility to her mother. Janine's face seemed immediately haggard with sorrow. She quickly whipped a strand of hair behind her ear.

"She told me about it," Linda murmured. "But I think it's just because she saw something of her own loneliness in me."

Janine furrowed her brow. How was it, she seemed to ask herself now, that Maggie had turned to this stranger for support? But rather than allow this silence to go on, Linda reached a hand between them and grabbed Janine's. Their eyes met.

"There is a whole lot of love in that girl," Linda said softly. "More love than in most people. In a way, speaking with her for the brief times we did was the gift of my trip to the Vineyard. I'll never forget her."

Janine swallowed but made no motion to stop touching Linda's hand.

"Maggie will have a baby in some way, be it adoption or some leap in science," Linda continued. "And she'll give that baby more love than most babies are allowed to have. I've thought about it endlessly since she told me. Especially because..." She trailed off as she furrowed her brow. "I left my baby. I left my child." A sob escaped her lips.

Janine's face was stricken for a split second before she righted it. "What happened? If you don't mind sharing."

Obviously, this was the deep, personal information Janine had been after all this time. Linda was terrified that she'd allowed this to spill out of her so easily.

"I never imagined that I'd settle down," Linda admitted

finally. "But when I met a man in Paris, I thought that finally, I'd found a fairytale all my own. We got pregnant almost immediately. And it wasn't until our baby was two years old or so that I realized he was cheating."

Janine, whose own husband had cheated, nodded with understanding.

"We lived in a culture I didn't fully understand. He was French, as were all of our friends. I found myself trying to stay above water with this language. I couldn't fully express myself, not my love nor my anger. Beyond that, money was tight, so when he didn't come home from work on time, I flew off the handle. We got into so many arguments. But his cruelty was unmatched. I felt that we were raising our daughter in an atmosphere of anger and resentment. And I began to really hate him for what he'd done to me. I felt like he'd trapped me there. I'd had this long list of things I'd wanted to do in my life."

Linda dropped her hand from Janine's as her eyes filled with tears. "One night, he became very violent. He gave me a black eye. I wasn't livid. I felt more resigned to the fact that... I just had to get out of there. I had to leave France. I had to become a different kind of person. But I had no money at all. I took a job far away and ran."

"Which meant you had to leave your child behind," Janine breathed.

Linda closed her eyes tightly as her shoulders shook. "She was only four, but I knew one thing for sure...that he would never lay a finger on our baby girl."

"And you've never had contact with her since then?"

Linda shook her head. "No. To be honest, I tried to shove all thought of her deep into the back of my mind for so many decades."

"That's understandable. You had to keep yourself alive in some way. And your husband created a terrible environment for you," Janine continued. "You couldn't stay there and stay sane for your child."

"Yes, but I should have gone back for her," Linda rasped. "I shouldn't have left her with that horrible man. It's not like a mother's love ever really goes away. I still feel it as strong and as powerful as I felt when she was very small. Gosh, I still think about those very early years. In some way, all my happiness was wrapped up in her. And it was some of the last happiness I ever experienced in my life."

Janine's shoulders sagged. "I'll tell you this. I'll tell you that your daughter's love for you is there, even if it's buried beneath years of resentment. My own mother left me in New York City years and years ago when I was only eighteen. I had to battle life on my own. Only in the past year have we mended our relationship."

"And you don't hate her?"

"Not even a little bit," Janine countered. "I don't know what my life would be without her. We need one another, especially right now. And, I understand why she did the things she did. I understand she was mentally ill and much younger, even, than I am now. When you left your daughter, you were probably no older than Maggie is right now."

"That's true," Linda whispered.

"And would you hold Maggie to the same standards that you now hold your past self?" Janine asked.

Linda shook her head. "No. I would give Maggie every form of forgiveness."

"Then practice that on yourself," Janine breathed. "Because you are so deserving of love and forgiveness. You are so deserving to move on from this."

"I don't know if I am," Linda countered. "You were nearly an adult when your mother left. My daughter was four. One day, her mother was gone. Imagine what that does to a person? Asking for forgiveness for that is like asking to go to the moon."

Linda stood and adjusted the tie of her robe. Her shoulders sagged forward horribly. She wondered if she would ever have the strength to walk upright again.

"Thank you for trying to help me, Dr. Grimson," she whispered. "But I'm afraid it's time for me to go."

Linda walked down the hallway as desolation took hold of her. Her heart beat slow, as though she was deep underwater. Very soon, she would return to her sad little rent-controlled apartment in the city and make peace with living out the rest of her life alone. This had been her last shot— and still more proof that she didn't deserve anything more than what she had.

Chapter Eighteen

aggie positioned her suitcase against the side wall of the house's foyer just as a message rang in from Rex on her cell.

REX: Let me know when you made it?

MAGGIE: I just walked in.

MAGGIE: I can't wait to have you here, too.

MAGGIE: Thank you for your support in all of this.

REX: We're stronger together. IVF ain't no thing.

REX: :)

"Is that a stranger?" Grandma Nancy stepped out from the bright lights of the kitchen with a mug of coffee lifted. She grinned sleepily as Maggie hustled over to her and burrowed her head in her grandmother's shoulder. Grandma Nancy eased a hand up and down her back, massaging it after the strain of the five-hour drive. "Let's get you some coffee, honey. Maxine and Janine are on the back porch."

Maggie poured herself a mug of piping-hot coffee as Grandma

Nancy sliced up a fresh loaf of bread from the Sunrise Cove Bistro's bakery and positioned them in the multi-slice toaster. "I have this fresh goat cheese and these figs…" Nancy positioned the beautiful purple fruits across a large platter with a shrug. "A light little early lunch for us until the rest of our crew returns home and demands a big afternoon meal."

"Let the Christmas eating commence!" Maggie teased.

Grandma Nancy laughed, although her eyes didn't match the sound. She folded and unfolded her hands on the counter. "Honey, are you doing all right? Your mother told me…"

Maggie grimaced. "We had our first doctor's appointment. It went well. Rex will start sticking me with needles in the New Year, which means I'll be a walking hormone monster. After that, I'll hopefully have enough eggs for a large beautiful harvest."

Nancy laughed appreciatively, although it seemed clear she couldn't fully understand. Grandma Nancy had gotten pregnant at sixteen and probably never imagined the great lengths some people had to go to make the "magic" happen. Maggie couldn't blame her for this. All she could do was be grateful for her support.

"Well, we love you, no matter how much of a hormone monster you'll become," Nancy said, just as the toast popped up in the toaster.

Maggie helped her grandmother load up the toast, refill mugs of coffee, and carry out the goat cheese and sliced figs. Maxine seemed in the middle of a giggle-fit as they crept out onto the porch. Janine's eyes filled with tears as she continued with her story.

"And you looked at that poor guy and said, 'I don't know what kind of party you think this is? But it's not the kind Maxine

Aubert would be caught dead at.' And then you opened his window and stepped out onto the fire escape!"

Maxine howled with laughter. "I can't believe I was ever so sassy."

"What? You can't believe it?" Grandma Nancy asked as she sat across from them. "Because that's just about all you were as a teenager, Max. Sassy and ready to fight."

Maxine's laughter calmed. She lifted her mug of coffee toward Grandma Nancy and then toward Maggie in greeting as Janine hopped up to give her daughter a big hug. Maggie nestled her head against her mother's shoulder and inhaled the beautiful scent of her perfume, something she'd taken in day after day, year after year. Perhaps someday, her own daughter would appreciate Maggie's scent. Perhaps it would be unquestioned, just as Janine's was.

The women sat for only a split-second before Janine confessed that, as it was noon and only a few days before Christmas, she would much prefer to switch to a "glass of rosé, at least," if the others were into it as well. Maxine agreed whole-heartedly as she spread goat cheese over her toast. Janine hopped up, headed inside, and reappeared with a bottle of locally sourced rosé. Just as she uncorked it, Maxine's phone blared.

"Oh gosh. It's Kelli!" Maxine cried. She lifted it and greeted the real estate agent who'd showed them a selection of houses across Martha's Vineyard. "Kelli, hi. I hope you have good news for me?"

Janine, Nancy, and Maggie gaped as Maxine's face erupted into a smile. "You know, that is some of the greatest news I've had in a very long time."

Maggie turned her eyes toward her mother to watch her own

emotions play out. Was Janine genuinely glad that her best-friend-turned-enemy-turned-best-friend-again had decided to move into her new world on the island? Was she really so good at forgiveness?

"She's going to come by here and bring the documents," Maxine said excitedly when she got off the phone.

"That's fantastic news!" Janine cried. "Gosh, it's happening!"

"It's empty, which means I can start the moving-in process as soon as I want to," Maxine explained in disbelief. "A real home on the ocean. My little Brooklyn eyes wouldn't have believed it."

"Which place is it?" Maggie asked.

"I think we saw it together," Maxine replied. "It was a bit too large for me, but I'm sure I'll find a way to fill it."

"You always said you wanted a dog or two," Janine countered.

Maxine laughed outright. "And lavish parties! Summer will be such a dream, won't it?"

"All our troubles will seem so far away..." Janine said, half-singing Beatles' lyrics.

Kelli arrived twenty-five minutes later, just as the women wrapped up their first glasses of wine and poured another. Maxine announced that there was every reason to celebrate. Maggie, for her part, was grateful to ease into the comfortable sounds of some of the women she loved the most. Even Maxine's joy was infectious.

"I brought the paperwork!" Kelli cried in greeting.

"And we've got some wine for you," Grandma Nancy said brightly. "Come. Sit with us."

They gave Kelli a chair around the back porch table. She clicked her pen and gazed out at the gorgeous surging ocean beyond, which lapped up against the cold sands of the long stretch of beach. Maxine leafed through the incredibly long document and muttered inwardly, sometimes switching over to French in a mocking way. "Oh la la," she teased.

Kelli laughed and sipped her glass of wine. "It's been such a pleasure hanging out with you through this process. It's not always so fun to take people around house-hunting."

"I'm sure it's sometimes a very thankless job," Janine interjected.

"Yes. I should have kept this house away from you, just to extend our time together a little longer," Kelli said with a laugh.

"Oh, come now, Cherie," Maxine said, still in that silly French accent. "Instead of being my realtor, you could just be my friend. I'm going to need a social circle beyond Janine, Maggie, and Nancy here on the island."

"I get it. We're just chopped liver to you," Nancy teased.

"Not so! I just have a very big house, and I need to fill it with loved ones," Maxine returned. "And besides, I've heard rumors that you've got yourself a pretty big family. I'll need them around for parties, too. Oh, and that boyfriend of yours! He's as cute as can be."

Kelli blushed. "He's a pretty new development." After a pause, she seemed to decide to spill the beans. "I was in a very abusive marriage for over twenty years. My new boyfriend has shown me that actually, there's a whole lot of love to be had in the world. I guess I never really understood that."

"Men can be just awful," Maxine whispered as her eyes darkened.

"I had a conversation with a client about her own abusive marriage," Janine confessed. "She left him years and years ago, and it still haunts her. I'm sure at the time that she felt the only way to sustain her mental health was to run as far as she could away from him. Ironically, her running away also destroyed her."

"That can happen," Kelli whispered. "I'm lucky that I have a really good support system. I'm somehow happier than I've been in my life. Not sure if I deserve it."

"Oh, mon Cherie. You deserve it," Maxine offered pointedly.

There was a strange moment of silence. Kelli's eyes swam with tears. In the distance, a seagull cawed dramatically, then swept over the beach, casting a long shadow.

"I meant to ask you, Maxine," Kelli continued. "This French accent you pull out sometimes. Is it fake?"

"Oh gosh," Janine teased. "She'll never drop it, will she?"

Maxine laughed outright. "I moved to the United States when I was eleven."

"So you're French?" Kelli asked.

"Half. My father was French. And my mother... well, I don't know much about her. She was American, so I guess that's how Dad got the visa for us to move over."

"She wasn't around?" Kelli furrowed her brow.

"No. She left us when I was four," Maxine admitted as her eyes grew shadowed. "I only know what my father told me. He was never a particularly nice man to have around. I took whatever he said with a grain of salt."

Janine's eyes widened the slightest bit. "What did he say?"

"Oh, Jan, I've told you all this," Maxine countered as she flashed her pen across the contract.

"I know. But tell me again," Janine breathed.

Maxine lifted her eyes to meet Janine's. "I told you. He said she was weak-minded and couldn't hack being a mother— that she couldn't deal with the French language. That she..."

"Do you know your mother's name?" Janine demanded suddenly.

Maxine's lips parted in surprise. "What? I've told you."

"I'm sure you have. But I've forgotten. She was never around. She was never a part of your story," Janine countered.

The air above the table had shifted strangely. Maggie turned her eyes from Janine to Maxine and back again as the two faced off.

"Janine? What the heck has gotten into you?" Nancy demanded.

Kelli sipped her wine as confusion made her eyes cloudy.

"Just tell me what her name is, Max," Janine breathed. "Please."

Maxine shrugged as she returned her eyes to her contract. "Her name was Linda. No idea what happened to her and I never bothered to look her up. I mean, she left me with a bastard of a father when I was four years old. Why should I care where that woman is? As far as I'm concerned, she's dead."

Chapter Nineteen

Maggie watched as Maxine spread out her fingers out on the back porch table, her eyes widened with shock. Her wine was untouched, and the contract remained unfinished. She'd just been told about the mysterious and sad woman named Linda up at the Lodge and the fact that her story lined up almost too well with Maxine's own.

How could any person grapple with that? Maggie wondered. The weight of it was immense.

Janine hustled back and forth, her cell pressed against her ear as she waited for Mallory to answer the phone. The sound of that name, Linda, still rang through the air over their table, and Maggie's heart seemed on the verge of explosion. Was it possible that the baby in Linda's photograph had been Maxine all this time? Was it possible that Linda had come to the Vineyard for some sort of last-ditch effort toward the love of family?

"Hi, Mallory. Yep, it's Janine. I wonder if you could tell me if our patient, Linda, has already checked out this afternoon?"

Janine stopped short in the midst of her manic pacing as she blinked back tears.

Maggie reached over and spread a hand over Maxine's. Maxine flinched but didn't move it. Beside Maggie, Kelli gulped her wine nervously, watching as the drama unfolded. Maggie wondered what other sorts of things you were allowed to see as a realtor. In many ways, you were overly-linked to people as they made enormous, life-altering decisions. Kelli must have seen so much.

"I remember her," Maxine breathed finally. "That older woman. So tired-looking. So lonely-looking."

Nancy leaned against the window of the porch with her arms crossed tightly over her chest. She looked incredulous. It was as though a bomb had just been dropped.

"You were close with her, weren't you?" Maxine asked Maggie softly. Her eyes shifted toward hers.

"We had a few conversations," Maggie affirmed. "She— she showed me an old photograph. Her and her husband and her baby."

Maxine's eyes shimmered. "I wouldn't have thought in a million years that my mother would have any regret for leaving. I thought she'd run out of France and never looked back."

"I think she's spent the past forty years looking back," Maggie countered. "It sounds to me like she's really hurt herself over the years, punishing herself."

"I wonder if she always knew it was me," Maxine whispered. "When Janine and I were in the tabloids..."

"It's possible that's how she found you," Grandma Nancy offered.

"All those years, I was listed as a Manhattan socialite in every trashy magazine," Maxine muttered. "I had no idea my mother was reading about me. I had no idea she existed on the same island as me. She could have been half the world away. And even the past few weeks... I looked her in the eye once. She stared at me in an almost scary way. I couldn't make any sense of it. I thought... I thought she was just a crazy old woman."

"Shoot. Okay." Janine spoke into the phone. "How long ago did she leave?"

Janine got off the phone and pressed it against her chest. "She checked out over an hour ago. One of the drivers took her to Oak Bluffs. It's possible that she's already left the island."

Maggie sprung toward the doorway that led from the closed-in porch to the kitchen. She felt an incredible amount of power and strength. She suddenly sensed what needed to be done— and knew in her heart that her happiness no longer mattered. She needed to find Linda. This Christmas, Linda needed to understand the weight of her family's love. She needed Maxine.

The other women were hot on her heels. There was a mad scramble for winter coats, hats, and gloves. Maggie rammed her feet into her boots as Janine jangled her car keys and hollered up to the upper floor for Alyssa, who appeared in a flash and performed a similar coat-glove-boot action. "What the heck is going on?" she demanded, which led to the rest of them speaking all at once to explain.

"That woman from the emergency room? The one who fainted?" Alyssa's eyes welled with curiosity. "I don't understand..."

Janine and Maxine hopped up front while Nancy, Alyssa, and Maggie crammed into the back. Kelli made them promise to tell her what happened the minute they found her, as she had several appointments to get to that afternoon.

"I'll process the contact for you, Maxine!" she hollered, just as all their doors slammed and Janine revved the engine.

"What a day," Grandma Nancy called as they rushed from the driveway and out onto the main road.

Snow swirled out from thick, grey clouds overhead. Alyssa slid her arm over Maggie's shoulder and shivered, seemingly with a mix of fear and excitement. The radio spat out Christmas tunes, one after the other, and they all seemed eerie and haunted.

"I just hope she hasn't left the island yet," Maxine breathed.

"I'm driving as fast as I can," Janine returned.

Once in Oak Bluffs, Janine parked just outside the ferry docks. A ferry buzzed alongside the nearest dock as several tourists scrambled on. A worker in a Santa hat accepted tickets and called, "Thank you for coming to the island! Merry Christmas, and have a safe trip back." Maggie's eyes traced down the long line of tourists but recognized no one.

Janine scrambled up toward the ticket-taker and asked if she could hop on to see if her friend was on the ferry. The ticket-taker shrugged "yes," and she jumped on. A minute later, she leaped off and shook her head at the others. After the tourists all boarded, Maggie listened as Janine spoke to the ticket-taker with more specificity, asking if an older woman of around sixty-five had boarded in the previous two hours. The man shrugged as Janine hunted for some proof of Linda's existence on her phone.

"Sometimes we have photographic records of our clients," she explained as she hunted. "But it looks like Linda never submitted anything of that kind."

Maggie furrowed her brow as chill overtook her. The sea looked tremendously volatile, like some kind of threat against their mission.

The ferry worker unraveled the ropes from the ferry to allow the large vessel its normal trek across the Vineyard Sound. Several tourists lined the outer edge of the boat and waved to the docks. One by one, Maggie, Alyssa, Maxine, Janine, and Grandma Nancy lifted their hands to wave in return. Maggie's heart pounded with sorrow. It seemed unlikely that they would ever find Linda. She hadn't even gotten around to asking after her Manhattan address.

When the ferry was too far for anyone to see them wave, Maxine burst into tears of confusion. Janine splayed a hand across her shoulder as Grandma Nancy leaped toward another worker to ask if they might look at the security footage to see if Linda had already gone through. Maggie turned to face the long line of surrounding shore, marveling at the confusion of a woman who'd looked her daughter in the eye for the first time in forty years and not known what to say.

"No wonder she was so lost," Janine whispered distractedly. "She found the answer and turned back. Maybe she thought you didn't need her after all."

Maxine sputtered with sorrow. "That's the thing, isn't it? Now that I know she was here, all I want in the world is to talk to her. I want to hear the full story. I've spent decades shoving the story as far away from myself as possible, not wanting to know why my mother did what she did. Now... if I never see her again... It's like losing her a second time. It's like losing all hope."

Chapter Twenty

An hour prior, Linda had purchased a ferry ticket and marched into the buzzing ferry with a heart as heavy as a rock in her chest. Once seated below deck, she'd reckoned with the weight of what had just occurred. She'd come to Martha's Vineyard, armed with the hope that seeing her daughter again would make her feel whole in a way she'd only ever dreamed of. But the sight of Maxine had filled her only with horror at her own failings. How could she possibly tell Maxine why she'd left when it no longer made sense to her? How could she look at that beautiful, powerful, rich forty-four-year-old woman and tell her why she'd destroyed her life forty years before?

Suddenly panicked, she'd nabbed her suitcase and rushed off the ferry just before its departure. She left her suitcase to the side of the deck and lifted her chin to a thick grey sky just as snow churned forth and peppered her cheeks and chin. Perhaps she just needed another few hours to live within the weight of her own longing. Perhaps she just needed another few hours to gaze out across the Vineyard Sound and dream her silly little dreams.

After all, it wasn't so difficult, sometimes, to envision just how different her life might have gone had she not left Maxine behind.

Perhaps she could have found a way to bring Maxine back to New York City with her. Perhaps she could have been a single mother, pinching pennies to get Maxine into ballet class or cheerleading. Perhaps she could have helped her through the strangeness of puberty or helped her pick out a dress for prom. Perhaps she could have mended her heart after her first big breakup or cooked her soup when she was sick.

In this reality, Maxine Aubert would never have met Janine Grimson. She would never have had the sort of friendship that transcended earthly love. But she also never would have had an affair with Jack Potter and ripped that family in two— something Linda had read about in the tabloids with a pain like a sword through her stomach.

Perhaps it was Linda's fault that Maxine had been so inwardly cold that she'd destroyed her best friend's marriage.

Why, then, had Janine and Maxine found a way to mend their relationship? This had struck Linda as especially strange. She'd never envisioned a reality in which forgiveness was such a given. She'd never imagined that anyone could ever forgive her for what she'd done.

Had she never done it, had she never left, she would never have stared into the colossal darkness of her loneliness, decade after decade. Everything would have been different. It was difficult for her to come to terms with the idea that this reality was the only one. She was sixty-five years old and nearing the end of her life.

Perhaps she had twenty years left— perhaps less. And what did she have to show for any of it?

She wandered from the dock and found her way to the water's edge. The Vineyard Sound frothed up near the toes of her scuffed boots. She stepped back just in time to avoid the harshness of damp socks. The snow, once so soft, now seemed torrential; it peppered her cheeks and her hair and made her shiver so much that it seemed her bones clacked together.

Why hadn't she been brave enough to tell Maxine she was her mother? How beautiful she'd looked that morning in the Lodge! Linda had felt a tremendous mountain of love for her. It was funny what love did to you. That very night, she'd found herself in an emergency room, surrounded by people she'd never known.

Maggie had gone away, just as Linda had known she would. She didn't blame the girl for moving on with her life. It was essential, especially at that age, to keep moving.

Linda continued to wander down the shoreline until she discovered a little collection of rocks. She collapsed upon the edge of one and held herself tightly into a ball. In the far-off distance, a sailboat breezed wildly through the whipping December winds. Who in their right mind sailed so deep into December? Who in their right mind sat on the frigid stones of a faraway beach? Who in their right mind went to an island far, far away to try to mend their relationship with a daughter who'd never really known them?

Years ago, at a job in California, a coworker had told Linda that she was too hard on herself. Linda hadn't known how to answer this. She'd wanted to explain just how little she deserved anything good due to her abandonment of her child.

Suddenly, a figure appeared far down the beach. Linda directed her nose toward the horizon and prayed that the man would pass her by without a single word of greeting. She'd wanted to be at a great distance from every human. She wanted nothing to do with banal small talk like, "Chilly today, isn't it?" or, "Getting close to Christmas!" It all felt so meaningless.

But when the figure neared her, she realized with a funny jolt in her stomach that she knew him. Joshua. The ferry boat captain from two weeks before. He no longer wore his ferry boat uniform and had bundled himself up in a thick red hat and a big, dark blue winter coat. He lifted a hand in greeting as his eyes found hers.

"Not used to anyone being out here on this stretch of beach," he told her in that same booming voice.

Linda kept her eyes on him as he approached. She felt unwilling to speak, although she knew that she needed to, if only to uphold some version of normality, even to herself. He got closer and stopped short as a slight smile wedged between his ears.

"I know you," he said finally. "It's not every day someone comes up to my cabin on the ferry."

Linda's throat tightened. She hadn't been recognized like this in decades; it seemed like.

"How was it at the Lodge?" he asked as he continued to march closer to her. His voice was fuzzy with familiarity, now. Linda wanted to wrap herself around and around with the sound of it, like a big scarf.

"Oh. The Lodge." Linda could hardly speak. She rubbed her palms together as chill overtook her.

Joshua lifted his thumb and pointed back toward the ferry docks. "I got a big pot of coffee waiting up there with our names on it if you're game. I don't know how long you've been sitting there, but if there's one thing I know about sitting around in the cold, it's that your body can't take it too long. Especially at our age."

Linda shook her head delicately. There was nothing in the world she wanted more, just then, than to share a pot of coffee with this handsome stranger. The universe couldn't allow it.

"What, then? You gonna stay out here all afternoon?" Joshua teased.

Sorrow overtook her. She curled her head forward so that her chin pressed against her chest. She willed him to leave; there was nothing for him, there— not conversation, not life—just a lonely woman with nothing to say for herself or her time on earth.

Finally, after an exasperated sigh, Joshua turned around and left her on that rock, just as she'd known he would do from the start. She laughed inwardly, but the laugh immediately dissipated in the wind. How ridiculous she was. She'd even left her suitcase on the docks as though nothing in her life was worthy of her care and attention.

Ten minutes later, there was the soft fall of footsteps through the sands. Linda lifted her chin the slightest bit to catch sight of Joshua, who carried two mugs of steaming coffee. His smile was strained, his motions slow. He lifted one of the mugs toward her and said, "If you won't come to the coffee, the coffee comes to you."

Linda could have burst into tears after that. She accepted the mug, wordless, and shifted over to allow Joshua to sit beside her on the rock. Together, they sipped the cooling coffee and gazed out at the waves. It felt like a dream Linda had had, something outside of time.

"I haven't been totally truthful about anything in my life," Linda finally spoke, surprising herself.

Joshua didn't speak. He nodded and sipped his coffee, prepared to listen.

"I came to the island because I knew my long-lost daughter was here," Linda continued softly. "I've watched her life through the pages of tabloid magazines, absolutely mesmerized with her beauty and her grace and her ability to leap through life without fear. She's made her mistakes, of course. And those mistakes have been well advertised in those same magazines. But I wept with compassion for her at every turn. And finally, when I realized that she'd come here, and I lost my job in the city, I felt that coming here to see her was my final shot at some kind of life."

"What happened when you saw her?" Joshua whispered, captivated.

Linda closed her eyes against the icy chill of the wind. "I chickened out. I couldn't understand why she would want me in her life. I would only complicate her already complicated existence. I would..."

But Joshua interrupted her.

"I don't know what happened in your life to lead you to this point. But you're deserving of love. Everyone is."

Linda turned her head so that their gazes met one another. Her heart thudded.

"This life is too cold to do it all by yourself," he continued. "And there's no telling what your daughter needs. Maybe she can't even imagine the amount of love you would bring into her world."

Linda had never envisioned the amount of perspective a stranger could bring into your world. She was captivated by his understanding, even if she didn't fully believe in it.

"Why don't we head back to the dock?" he suggested. "I just have to make a few runs to Falmouth and then I'm home free for the afternoon. We can continue this conversation in a warm place. Or, we don't have to talk about anything at all."

Linda's smile was so slight that she could hardly feel it. "I would like that."

Chapter Twenty-One

Linda and Joshua headed back to the dock. They walked with three feet separating them as the colossal winds rushed against their winter coats and ripped into Linda's hair. She felt so tired, as though all her years of improper nutrition had waited for this moment to take her down.

About fifty feet from the dock, Linda lifted her eyes to catch sight of two familiar beauties standing at the far end of the dock, their heads bent as they conversed. Janine Grimson and Maxine Aubert. It was as though they'd stepped out of the pages of a tabloid magazine, becoming a kind of mirage. Linda stopped short and gaped at them, which led Joshua's eyes toward them, as well.

"Don't tell me that's her," he whispered.

"You see her, too?"

"The blonde one. Right?"

Linda nodded, unable to find her voice enough to speak. She spread her hand over her heart and suddenly envisioned Maxine as a younger version of Linda herself— frightened of whatever else awaited her in middle age, especially as her depression became like a great ocean, threatening to overtake her. Joshua lifted a hand to wave toward the two women, which caught Janine's attention almost immediately. Linda wanted to scold him for this. She wasn't sure she was ready. Perhaps she never would be.

Janine placed a hand over her brow and gazed out at Linda and Joshua. Her lips formed a round O of surprise. Maxine followed her gaze, looking stricken. After a strange moment's pause, she hustled forward, so that her blonde hair swept back behind her. She ran toward Linda, her legs long and whipping out behind her and the sand kicking up. Linda's heart thudded with fear and longing.

Years and years ago, Linda had watched, captivated, as her daughter had taken her first steps across the living room in their apartment in the nineteenth arrondissement. She'd hobbled and then fallen onto the pad of her diaper. Her eyes had glowed with pure joy as Linda had told her, over and over again, just what a big girl she now was.

Maxine stopped her wild sprint about five feet away from Linda and Joshua, who stood with bated breath. Maxine slid a strand of hair behind her ear as she gaped at Linda.

How was this possible? How had Maxine figured this out?

"Is it really you?" Maxine whispered as her eyes welled with tears.

Linda tightened her hand over her chest. How could she find the strength to speak? She'd dreamed of this moment for years and here it was before her. Would she mess this up, too? How could she trust herself?

"It's me," Linda finally murmured. "It's really me."

Maxine looked frozen with shock. Janine appeared behind

her, similarly wild with confusion. Far behind them, Maggie stood with another young woman and Nancy. Both watched, captivated.

"Why didn't you tell me?" Maxine whispered as she stepped closer.

"I was terrified," Linda answered truthfully. "And I'm still terrified."

Linda shivered so frantically that her teeth clacked together. She stepped ever-so-slightly toward her daughter, which made her knees nearly collapse beneath her. Maxine leaped forward and gripped Linda's arm to keep her upright.

"We'd better get her to a warm place," Joshua said in that booming voice. "She's been outside for a long while."

Linda placed her head upon Maxine's chest and allowed herself to be led toward the docks. The stress and the chill had created a strange, muffled noise within her head. In many ways, this all seemed like a dream. She prayed she wouldn't wake up in her New York apartment a few minutes later. She prayed this was real.

Voices continued above her head as she shuffled toward the parking lot alongside the docks.

"I can make up the guest bedroom," Janine offered.

"She'll be comfortable with us," Maggie said brightly.

"I don't know..." Maxine doubted, her voice heavy with doubt. "It might be overwhelming for her. All those people in one place..."

A car door opened as Maxine's voice coaxed Linda to slide in and buckle her seatbelt. When she did, she peered out the door to find Maxine, Janine, and Joshua in a line, all peering down at her. She felt like a little kid.

"You're going to be all right, Linda," Joshua said firmly. "You're with family now."

Linda blinked back tears as Joshua leafed through his pockets and dragged out a little yellow pad of paper. He waved it around like a flag and said, "I don't have my cell phone on me. I never got used to it, but if I give you my number, will you give me a call? Just want to make sure you're all right."

Linda's heart jumped into her throat. When was the last time a man had asked for her phone number? This wasn't that; there was no flirtation in his asking after her, a genuine crazy person.

Or was there? Linda couldn't figure out anything any longer.

Joshua scribbled his cell phone number onto the pad of paper as Maxine, Nancy, Maggie, another young woman, and Janine all jumped in the car. Janine revved the engine as Joshua handed her his number, and closed the door behind her, tucking her in safe from the howling winds.

"Looking forward to seeing you again soon, Linda. I hope you enjoy the holidays here on the island. If I had to guess, I don't think you're headed back home any time soon."

Chapter Twenty-Two

The following morning, Maggie's eyes fluttered open as the sound of laughter cascaded up the staircase. She rolled over to spot Alyssa, who was all tucked away beneath her comforter. Incredibly, it was December 20th — only six weeks since Jack Potter's death. It seemed that with every passing day, the world around them shifted so incredibly that it was no longer recognizable.

Case in point: the mysterious and lonely woman at the Lodge had been Maxine's mother all along.

Maggie tip-toed to the bathroom to scrub her face and don the slightest bit of mascara and lip gloss. She then charged downstairs to find Nancy, Carmella, Elsa, and Janine in the midst of a wild conversation about the previous day's events. A big box of Frosted Delights donuts sat between them, wide open. Maggie's stomach grumbled even as a small voice in the back of her head told her to resist. (She would ignore this voice. It was Christmas, after all.)

"I've been working with her for two weeks," Janine breathed over her mug of coffee. "She never mentioned it to me once."

"That's insane," Carmella returned as she lifted a big chocolate-covered donut and tore out a large bite.

"I haven't heard a peep from her all morning," Nancy said as she placed her hands on her hips. "I hope she knows she's welcome here as long as she likes."

"What about Maxine?" Elsa demanded. She'd missed the majority of the events the previous day as she'd spent the afternoon and evening with Bruce, while Carmella had been off somewhere with Cody and Gretchen.

"Maxine is overwhelmed, to say the least," Janine affirmed. "She was all but catatonic when we got back yesterday. We drank a few glasses of wine until maybe nine or nine-thirty and then she passed out in another guest bedroom."

"So you're saying both mother and daughter are in this house right now?" Carmella breathed. There was a small crumb of donut on her lower lip, but nobody pointed it out.

"Poor Linda," Maggie spoke for the first time, which forced everyone to notice her as she slipped onto a chair alongside the dining room table and assessed the many donut varieties. "She seems just about as lost as anyone I've ever known."

The other women considered her words as Maggie selected a caramel-flavored donut and took a decadent bite. Janine collapsed in the chair across from her and placed her head in her hands.

"What did Maxine tell you about her mother when you two were growing up?" Elsa asked as she poured herself another cup of coffee.

Janine pursed her lips. "She didn't speak about her often. But she did say..." She shook her head delicately. "She said that if she'd been her mother, she would have left her father, too. Maxine wasn't exactly a fan of him. He's been dead a long time, but even I can't imagine being married to him."

There was silence. Carmella's eyes widened as Elsa flicked off the little piece of donut on Carmella's lower lip.

"And this coming from the woman who married Jack Potter. I know what you're all thinking," Janine said with a heavy sigh.

"Nobody said that honey," Nancy countered.

"Yes, but I can't help but think about it. All the patterns of abuse. They're generational," Janine murmured. She then turned her eyes toward Maggie as she added, "And then there's my beautiful daughter, who's married a decent man."

"Not just decent," Maggie replied firmly.

"That's the voice of love right there," Elsa said warmly.

"Speak of the devil. Isn't he supposed to be on the Vineyard today?" Nancy asked.

"That's right. He should be here by lunchtime," Maggie said, surprised at her level of excitement.

"I hope he brought enough gifts for everyone," Nancy teased. "We're a greedy bunch."

"Tiffany necklaces for all." Maggie laughed outright as Grandma Nancy winked.

"I realized we don't have a single Christmas cookie in this house," Janine said suddenly. "We'd better get to baking if we're ever going to welcome so many people into the house for Christmas. Lemon bars, cut-outs, buckeyes... We have our work cut out for us."

"Put me to work, captain," Carmella teased.

Janine bustled around the kitchen to collect the measuring cups and big mixing bowls. Nancy turned on the radio to another

Christmas station while Elsa began to make another of her classic lists. As Janine poured the first round of flour, Maxine appeared in the doorway in one of Janine's nightgowns. She stretched her arms up over her head as a yawn broke between her cheeks.

"There she is," Janine greeted warmly.

"Rumor has it you had quite the weekend," Carmella affirmed.

Maxine stepped into the kitchen, grabbed one of the bottles of Bailey's, and poured herself a stiff coffee drink. She puffed out her cheeks as she sipped the first of what would probably be many sips that morning, her eyes cast out toward the blustery ocean.

"My mother is here. In this house," she murmured with disbelief.

"We can't believe it," Nancy shook her head.

Maxine turned her eyes toward Nancy. "You were my stand-in mother in Brooklyn. All those years."

Nancy scoffed with embarrassment. "I wasn't much of anything."

"But you were there," Maxine affirmed.

They'd entered strange territory. Janine poured the rest of the dry ingredients together in a mixing bowl and began to stir furiously. Nobody knew what to say.

But finally, Maxine found the words.

"I've been so awful in my life," she murmured. "So, so awful, in ways I'll never be able to completely forgive myself. I can see that in my mother's eyes, too."

"Oh, honey. You shouldn't—" Nancy began.

"No. I have to," Maxine countered. "I've already counted my blessings ten-fold to be allowed to live alongside all of you here on the Vineyard after what I did. I've been given so much and now a second chance. Now, I have to pass along that giving to none other than Linda— my mother. I never imagined in a million years..."

She sipped the Bailey's once more, her eyes shadowed with disbelief.

"What do you plan to do?" Carmella asked.

Maxine heaved a sigh. "I've just signed the contract to buy that large house on the edge of the beach. It had too much space for me. But maybe... Maybe it has just enough space for me and the mother I never knew. We have a whole lot of metaphorical baggage to move in there with us."

Maggie's lips parted with surprise.

Linda. Lonely, terrified Linda, who hadn't had a day of happiness in forty years.

Linda would have a place to go home to.

An hour or so later, Rex arrived, just as Alyssa finally got out of bed and faced the world. Maggie leaped into Rex's arms and he swung her around and around the living room, so much so that Elsa scolded them. "You're going to hit the Christmas tree, and then where will we be?"

Carmella laughed outright at that. "Elsa. Lighten up! The kids are happy to see each other."

"Kids? How old are they again?" Alyssa scoffed. "I can see your crow's feet from here," she teased Maggie.

"Get out of here," Maggie returned to Alyssa as she grinned up at Rex, her heart swelling with adoration. "You're finally here!" she whispered to Rex.

"Just in time for cookies," Alyssa countered. "That's so typical, Rex."

"Glad to see you haven't changed at all, Alyssa," Rex returned.

"There's no changing perfection," Alyssa offered with the flip of her hair.

"Guys! The first batch of cookies are ready to frost!" Janine hollered from the kitchen. "I need all hands on deck."

Alyssa yawned and headed off to the kitchen as Maggie, Rex, and Carmella followed in after her. Carmella poured them all glasses of wine as Maxine hovered over the architectural plans for the house she'd just purchased.

"I think I'll take this bedroom and give Linda this one," she said to Janine, pointing them out. "And this room could be the library? I'll, of course, need your help with interior decorating."

"Just like old times," Janine said with a laugh. "Remember that fight we got into about the redesign of my kitchen? I swear, I couldn't understand what you meant when you said that wallpaper wouldn't work. And then we got it up..."

"It looked like a nightmare room," Alyssa confirmed as she slid the first of the frosting over a reindeer-shaped cookie. "I remember that."

Maxine tossed her head back with laughter. "Yes, that was a misfire. But almost every other room we've designed together was a huge hit."

"I can remember when the two of you would decorate Janine's bedroom during sleepovers," Nancy said. "Those big fairy tents and all those light-up stars..."

"We were obsessed with making every space a kind of fantasy," Janine murmured thoughtfully.

"And I suppose that's what I want this place to be for Linda," Maxine said as her brow furrowed. "I want it to be a fantasy, in a way. But I also want it to feel like home."

"She'll be with you, honey," Grandma Nancy affirmed. "You're her home."

Chapter Twenty-Three

Decември 24th, Christmas Eve. The date came out of Linda's pen as she scribed in her diary, poised at a little table Maxine had set up for her in the bedroom that was now, for whatever reason, hers.

December 24th, 2021

It's hard to believe that I find myself here.

For decades, Maxine was nothing but a ghost to me. She haunted me from the pages of tabloid magazines; she seemed a portrait of fashion, life, vitality, and beauty— all things that I'd never fully ascribed to myself.

Now, Maxine has asked me to live with her in this huge house at the side of the sea while she makes plans to officially leave the city for good.

Our conversations remain strained. It's not as though you can just snap your fingers and make everything right as rain, not after so much time apart. We eat meals together, drink coffee, and sometimes even open a bottle of wine. She's opened up briefly about how guilty she still feels about her affair with Jack Potter.

"I still can't believe he's dead," she told me last night. "I don't want to be glad that anyone is dead. And I'm not. But I'm so, so glad to have Janine back. I don't know why I deserve the love she's given me. I don't know why I deserve Martha's Vineyard. But I picture it as a new start. For all of us. Including you, Linda."

I suppose it will take a long, long time before she's up to calling me "mom." Maybe she never will be.

Linda leaned back and blinked out the large window, with its near-perfect view of the frothing ocean. Her bedroom remained sparse, with only a table and a queen-sized bed behind her. The window didn't yet have curtains; although she wasn't quite sure she wanted them. Back in Manhattan, her view of the city below had filled her with a sense of dread, as it had been a near-constant reminder of the world she didn't inhabit and all the relationships she didn't have. Now, her window showed the Atlantic Ocean, a seemingly monstrous and beautiful thing of countless stories and future possibilities.

Maybe she had entered a new phase of her life— one without fears. One with only beautiful possibilities. One of love.

Suddenly, there was a horrible, piercing beeping noise. Linda burst up from her chair and rushed down the hallway toward the kitchen, the source of the sound. There, Maxine stood on a chair and peered at the beeping smoke alarm. She wore a light pink robe and a pair of fuzzy slippers, a funny contrast to her grunting and cursing at the alarm.

The source of the smoke was the stovetop, where it looked like Maxine had begun a Christmas Eve dinner and subsequently burnt it. Linda stepped toward the blackening sauce and removed it from the heat as Maxine finally cut out the beeping noise.

"Gosh, I'm so sorry!" Maxine said nervously as she stepped down from the chair.

"Don't worry yourself!" Linda said, still feeling as though Maxine was a stranger. "What were you up to in here, anyway?"

"I wanted to surprise you with Christmas Eve dinner," Maxine replied, wrinkling her nose. "But I screwed it up."

Linda burst into laughter. "You shouldn't worry about that." How could she explain to her daughter that she'd hardly had a nice meal in two decades?

"I wanted to make you feel like... like this was your home," Maxine continued.

Linda looked at her daughter with compassion. "Honey, it's going to take time. For both of us."

"I know that," Maxine returned.

Their eyes found one another as they stirred with a mix of sorrow and hope.

"I should have known I couldn't cook," Maxine said finally as her face erupted into a smile.

"Maybe we can learn together," Linda suggested.

Maxine nodded as she lifted the skillet and placed it beneath the sink. "We have a whole lot to learn together, I think."

That moment, Linda's phone buzzed from her pocket. She lifted it to find another text from that beautiful ferry boat captain,

Joshua, who now wished her a Merry Christmas Eve. Linda's heart thudded. She no longer recognized her life.

On cue, Maxine's phone buzzed. "Janine says they've made too much food for Christmas Eve dinner. They want us to come over."

"And what do you think about that?" Linda asked.

Maxine pressed her lips together as she shivered with nervous laughter. "I think she probably already knew I was going to mess up dinner."

"It's good to have friends who know you," Linda said firmly.

Maxine cocked her head as her smile grew. "And it's good to have a mother around, too."

Linda's heart lifted. When Maxine had first told her about this arrangement, that she wanted Linda to move in with her, she'd ached with doubt. How could they mend all the trauma from their past? How could they see eye-to-eye?

But with each passing moment, they seemed to both recognize the truth: that there was no "mending" trauma. There was only acceptance of the past and a push forward for something new, beautiful, and whole.

And what better place to do it than right there?

Linda showered and dressed in a Christmas vest and a pair of black slacks. Maxine donned a glittery black dress, something she said she'd worn previously to a high-rollers Christmas party in Manhattan.

"I know it might be a bit too much," Maxine started with a funny smile. "But I have to wear my clothes somewhere. I can't just let them sit in my closet, unused."

Outside, a thick blanket of snow shimmered over the dark landscape, stretching out toward the frothing ocean and across the rolling hills toward the woods just beyond. Linda leaped into the front seat of Maxine's BMW, recently purchased, and watched as Maxine buckled herself in safely. Still, they hadn't had all the conversations they needed to have. Still, there was a heaviness between them— an expectation that soon, they would have to stare at the darkness between them and consider how to make this work.

As they pulled into the driveway of Janine, Nancy, Elsa, Carmella, Maggie, and Alyssa's house, Linda heaved a sigh and slid her palms over her thighs.

"What is it?" Maxine asked as she turned off the engine.

Linda hesitated for a long, long time before she spoke.

And this time, when she spoke, she spoke in French as a way to unite them back to the past they shared.

"Je regrette tout," she whispered. (Which meant, "I regret everything.")

"Ne pas," Maxine returned softly. She lifted a hand to Linda's and squeezed it gently.

"I still remember the last time I saw you before I left," Linda breathed. "You were wearing a little blue sailor's dress. You'd made me a picture, which I lost somewhere in China."

Maxine's eyes widened with surprise at the memory. "I don't have so many images of you, Linda."

"You were so little."

"But I do remember the way you smelled," Maxine breathed, interrupting her. "And when I first found you that afternoon on the beach and I helped you to Janine's car, that smell took me all the way back to Paris. It took me back to another life. And it reminded me of the immensity of my love for you. It never really went away. I don't suppose it ever will."

～

The table was stuffed to the gills with Christmas Eve dinner— a roasted turkey, stuffing, bright red cranberries, homemade rolls, mashed potatoes and turnip, and several different kinds of pies and Christmas cookies.

"You all know that we can still eat tomorrow, right? Today's only Christmas Eve," Carmella teased them as they sat around the table.

Linda sat off to the side, next to Maxine, feeling like a sort of outcast. Maggie sat alongside a handsome man in his twenties. Their hands were latched together under the table and they gave one another secretive glances. Linda prayed with her heart of hearts that one day soon, the beautiful married couple would find a way to become parents. They deserved it. The love they shared bubbled around them, an aura the rest of them could feel easily.

Maggie's eyes found Linda's over the table. They hadn't yet had the time to speak, as Linda and Maxine had only just arrived. Linda felt sheepish and strange. Did Maggie think she was a fool?

"Linda. I'm so glad you're here," Maggie whispered, just loud enough for Linda to hear as the chorus of other Christmas revelers echoed from wall to wall in the beautiful dining room. "Merry Christmas."

"Merry Christmas to you, Maggie," Linda returned as her eyes welled with tears. "I can't tell you enough how much your kindness meant to me. It made me feel less alone for the first time in decades."

Maxine placed a hand over Linda's shoulder as Janine rose to lift a glass of champagne over the rest of them.

"I can't even begin to say what this Christmas means to me,"

Janine offered finally, her voice cracking. "All I know is that each and every one of you holds a very special place in my heart. The rest of our lives will look a whole lot different after this year. And I suppose we can only be grateful for it. Merry Christmas. To all of you."

Every person at the table— from Elsa's children, Alexie and Cole and Mallory, to Janine's children, Maggie and Alyssa, to Carmella and her fiancé, Cody and his young child, Gretchen, along with Bruce and Henry, lifted their sparkling glasses of champagne with assurance. Maxine and Linda joined them. Christmas ghosts seemed to surround them— everyone from Elsa's husband to Nancy's husband to Jack Potter.

But that was the thing about Christmas. It was haunted with endless memories— yet powerful enough to allow you to make countless new ones. Linda's heart ached with longing, but this time, the life she longed for was the one she now lived. How lucky she felt. It was perhaps too good to be true.

∾

Coming Next in the Katama Bay Series

Pre Order New Beginnings

Other Books by Katie

The Vineyard Sunset Series

Sisters of Edgartown Series

Secrets of Mackinac Island Series

A Katama Bay Series

Mount Desert Island Series

Connect with Katie Winters

BookBub: www.bookbub.com/authors/katie-winters
Amazon: www.amazon.com/Katie-Winters/e/B08B1S7BBN
Facebook: www.facebook.com/authorkatiewinters/
Newsletter: www.subscribepage.com/kwsiguppage

To receive exclusive updates from Katie Winters please sign up to be on her Newsletter!

www.subscribepage.com/kwsiguppage

Made in the USA
Monee, IL
02 September 2022

13070702R10115